SHAR

The Dark
TOWER

cover art by
Ginette Beaulieu

Scholastic Canada Ltd.

Scholastic Canada Ltd.
123 Newkirk Road, Richmond Hill, Ontario, Canada L4C 3G5

Scholastic Inc.
555 Broadway, New York, NY 10012, USA

Scholastic Australia Pty Limited
PO Box 579, Gosford, NSW 2250, Australia

Scholastic New Zealand Limited
Private Bag 94407, Greenmount, Auckland, New Zealand

Scholastic Ltd.
Villiers House, Clarendon Avenue, Leamington Spa,
Warwickshire CV32 5PR, UK

Canadian Cataloguing in Publication Data

Stewart, Sharon (Sharon Roberta), 1944-
The dark tower

ISBN 0-590-12438-2

I. Title.

PS8587.T4895D37 1998   jC813'.54   C97-931852-1
PZ7.S73Da 1998

5 4 3 2 1   Printed in Canada   8 9 /9 0 1 2 /0

To M.T.C., who wouldn't have wanted it.
To R.J.S., who always did.
S.S.

This novel is a work of fiction. Although it is based on the life of Marie Thérèse Charlotte de France, some characters, events and details have been altered in the interests of the story.

October 1795

They want me to remember everything that happened, and write it all down. Do they think I could forget any of it? Mon dieu, do they think I don't wake up in the dark of night, remembering? And why write it all down now? Because they plan to do to me what they did to the others? Or do I only feel afraid because it is so cold, and still raining, and the wind always sounds so mournful around the Tower?

Well, I will give them the account they want. Why not? They've kept me locked up and silent long enough. So I will write of the events I remember, and the facts I know. That will satisfy them.

But my own deepest feelings I will not tell them. Let them guess, if they will. Not for them this story, the real story, of our long journey from sunshine into shadow . . .

1

Sorrows

June 1789

My name is Marie Thérèse Charlotte de France, and I am a princess. I suppose I'm not the usual sort of princess. For one thing, I am not charming. Princesses are supposed to be, of course. Beautiful and charming and accomplished. Well, I am none of those things, and I know it.

My maman, Queen Marie Antoinette, used to tell me at least once a day that pride was my worst fault. Yet what had I been told all my life? That I was descended from famous ancestors going back a thousand years. That my papa, King Louis XVI, ruled the most glorious country in Europe, and that Versailles, the palace I lived in, was the most splendid in the whole world. So how could I help being proud?

Yet despite my pride, I had many Sorrows. One was the Sorrow of Being Born a Girl, for this meant I could never rule France. There was a law against it. That's why my brother Charles was the Dauphin, heir to the throne, although he was only four. Another of them was the Sorrow of Shortness. Everyone in the world, except for my little brother, was taller than I was. I spent all my time with my neck cricked back, looking up at people. This may have helped with the pride a bit, but it was no help to my temper.

Even this, though, was nothing compared to the Sorrow of Etiquette. My governess, the old macaw . . .

But I'd better explain about my game. People remind me of animals, so the first thing I do when I meet someone new is decide which animal it is. I did it with all the people around me. My governess, Madame de Mackau, with her beaky nose and shrewd beady eyes, looked exactly like a macaw. I knew because I'd seen a picture of one in a book of Papa's. I never called her that to her face, of course. I was too much in awe of her for that. But I sometimes did behind her back, which I suppose was wicked of me. Dear, kind Madame de Fréminville, my *femme de chambre*, was a different kind of animal. Frémi had round eyes and a habit of twitching her nose. A perfect rabbit. I did call her that sometimes, just to tease her.

My own family were animals too, of course, though I would never have dared to tell them so. Maman, the Queen, was tall and beautiful, with golden hair and bright blue eyes. She had a long snowy neck, and a smooth gliding walk. I thought she was as graceful as a swan. My papa, though, was stout and a little awkward in his movements. He was a bear. Not a ferocious bear, but a kindly, shambling one. Charles, my clever little brother, was definitely a squirrel – mischievous and full of tricks.

As for me, I was a pony, a mettlesome pony that people were always trying to put a bridle on. The bridle was called etiquette. Princesses are never allowed just to *be*. There's always something they're supposed to be thinking or not thinking, doing or not doing, every single minute of the day. "Stand up straight!" they tell you. But not so straight that people think you are stiff. "Be responsive!" But never show your feelings. "Smile!" But not too much, and never grin. "Curtsey or nod to all the right people!" But never, ever to the wrong people. There are a couple of thousand other rules like that, and I was supposed to remember all of them.

The macaw used to say that etiquette is your backbone. It gives you support from the inside. Maman always said it's a suit of armour: heavy to wear, but it gives a lot of protection. All I knew was, I never got it right. Maybe that's why my family always called me Mousseline, which means "fluffy." It was supposed to refer to my frizzy hair, but sometimes I think they meant my brains as well.

That summer of 1789, when everything in my life began to change forever, I was eleven. It was late June, the hottest anyone could remember, and already the heat was fraying people's tempers. As usual, I was struggling with etiquette.

"I won't wear it!" I glowered down at the puffy

white dress the wardrobe maids had laid out on my bed. "It makes me look like a . . . a sheep! I want to wear the blue one. The one with the *paniers*. Please, Frémi."

Madame de Fréminville rolled her eyes. "Your Highness, you know the blue satin isn't suitable. Not for today. It's much too heavy for such hot weather, and the *paniers* are too formal."

"But we're dining in public, and I hardly ever get to wear the blue. And it's my favourite."

"Madame de Mackau won't approve . . ."

Of course she wouldn't. The macaw hardly ever approved of anything I did. It made me want to wear the dress even more. "*Pleeease*, Frémi."

I could tell Frémi was beginning to weaken. She usually did when I worked on her enough. "*Parbleu*, Frémi," I said, "What can the old macaw do, after all. Peck us to death?"

Frémi smothered a smile. She did try to be proper all the time, but she couldn't quite manage it. It was the thing I liked best about her. She nodded to the maids. The white muslin dress was carried off, and the blue satin unwrapped from its green taffeta cover and brought forward.

Someday, I promised myself, I shall have as many gowns as Maman, and every single one will have *paniers*.

I had to take a deep breath and hold it in as the maids laced my stays tightly up the back over my chemise and petticoat. Then the *paniers* were fastened with ribbons to the bottom of the stays, one on each side, like baskets. The dress followed. I stood before the mirror, swishing my skirts, admiring the way the basketwork held the shining folds out on each side. Mine were only little *paniers*, of course. On grand occasions, Maman and the great ladies of the court wore ones so wide that they had to go through doors sideways.

"Isn't it lovely?" I crowed.

No one answered. I glanced over my shoulder and there in the doorway was Madame de Mackau! I quickly turned back to the mirror, trying to pretend I hadn't seen her. It was all very well to joke about her when she wasn't there. In the flesh, she could freeze me to the spot.

"What on earth!" she exclaimed. "Madame de Fréminville, what can you be thinking of? *Paniers*, today? And heavy satin in this hot weather?"

"Don't scold Frémi," I said quickly. "It's my fault. She didn't want me to wear it, but I insisted."

"Your Highness is too old for such nonsense. Please take it off at once!"

Now, I don't like being given orders. So I folded my arms and refused to budge.

Frémi glanced at the clock on the mantel. "Madame, there really isn't time for her to change now," she pleaded. "There's her hair still to be done and it's past eleven thirty. She mustn't be late for mass."

Madame de Mackau frowned and bit her lower lip. She was beaten, and she knew it. I certainly couldn't be late for mass. It simply wasn't proper etiquette. *Too bad!*

"Oh, very well," she snapped. "But heaven knows what Her Majesty will say!"

Having won my point, I stood still, for once, while the maids combed my frizzy hair into curls, powdered it white, and wound blue ribbons through it to match the dress. I took one last look in the mirror. Maybe it wasn't the right dress for today. But, oh, it was beautiful.

Followed by Madame de Mackau and two ladies in waiting, I hurried up the stairs that led to the Queen's Apartments on the floor above. My mother was ready and waiting – and Maman didn't like to be kept waiting. Charles was already there, attended by the ladies and gentlemen of his household. He had far more people to wait upon him than I did, and much finer rooms, too. He gave me a big smile, probably because he knew I'd be in trouble for keeping Maman waiting.

I curtsied carefully to her, making sure not to catch my heel in the hem of my gown, and trying not to wobble on the way up.

She was looking very splendid in her new silk dress. Its pinkish brown shade was all the fashion at court that year. Papa had joked that it was exactly the colour of a flea. He was right, but Maman had not been amused.

She wasn't amused now, either. The expression in her eyes was stony as they travelled first over me and then, questioningly, to Madame de Mackau. She couldn't say anything about my dress now, of course. That wouldn't have been proper etiquette in the midst of a crowd of ladies and gentlemen. So I was safe for the moment. I crossed my fingers behind my back. With any luck, Maman might forget to scold me later.

Without a word, she turned and led the way toward the royal chapel, which lay on the far side of the palace. Her ladies-in-waiting fell in behind her. Her friend, the stuck-up Yolande de Polignac, came next, leading my brother Charles by the hand. His ladies and gentlemen followed. Madame de Mackau and my two ladies followed me at the end of the procession.

At the south end of the palace we emerged into the Hall of Mirrors. Late morning sun poured through the tall arcaded windows that ran the length of the huge gallery, glancing off the mirrored walls opposite and the huge crystal and silver chandeliers overhead. Rich carpets in scarlet and blue, and red marble columns capped with gold, glowed in the dazzling light. I always liked the Hall – it was like walking into a rainbow.

Down the length of the gallery people stood about in groups, some waiting to see us pass by on our way to the chapel, others just there to gape at everything. For it was the custom that anyone decently dressed and not freshly marked by the smallpox might visit the public rooms of Papa's palace of Versailles. Like all of us, it too belonged to France.

A whisper ran before us. "It's the Queen! The

Queen, and Monsieur le Dauphin!" Courtiers bowed and curtsied, like a bed of brightly coloured flowers bending in the wind. Other folk, not used to the ways of the court, craned their necks to see us pass. Maman nodded graciously to left and right as she glided along. Charles, too, smiled and nodded. He was very good at it, but then, *he* had plenty of charm.

🌿 🌿 🌿

After mass, Papa, Maman and the rest of us trailed back across the palace to Maman's apartments, where we would dine in public. Despite the sunshine outside, the room was ablaze with candles. Their light gleamed on silver cutlery and sparkled off cut-crystal goblets, and their heat made the air shimmer and dance. Sweat trickled down between my shoulder-blades under the heavy satin of my bodice. I was beginning to regret not wearing the muslin gown.

I gazed down at the steaming plate of soup in front of me and sighed. Maman glanced down the table at me, and the message in her eyes was clear. "Eat something!" So I picked up my spoon and swallowed a mouthful. Who could possibly want to eat soup on such a hot day? And why would anybody want to watch someone else do it?

Yet the room was half full of people, and the eyes of all of them were riveted on us. Part of the room was cordoned off, and behind the purple velvet ropes a crowd stood many ranks deep to see Papa and the rest of us eat our meal. They whispered, pointed, tittered behind their hands, and strained their ears to hear any tidbits of conversation we might exchange. There were silk-clad courtiers, and portly merchants in sober dark colours. You could tell which of these had only rented their formal swords at the gate – they looked as if they might trip over them. There were plain working folk too, the men clad in clean cotton smocks, the women with crisp white kerchiefs at their necks and aprons over their best dresses.

Eating in public always made me feel like an animal in the palace zoo. I knew it was my duty, but it was a horrible one. How my parents stood it, I never knew. Charles and I only dined in public twice a week, but my parents did it almost every day.

I sneaked a glance down the table. Maman, as usual, was eating very little, but Papa was placidly spooning up his soup. He was the only one who ever really enjoyed any of these dinners. The truth was, all of us usually had a small snack beforehand, so most of the food ended up being distributed to the servants, and to any of the poor who came to the doors of the palace kitchens. Still, we had to eat a little. Watching us chewing and swallowing was part of the show, and people expected it.

The delicate soup plates were whisked away by white-gloved servants, their foreheads beaded with sweat under the snowy white of their wigs. As platters laden with the next course were carried in, there was a stir and scuffle amongst the crowd, as people who wanted to leave scrambled rudely over those at the back who had just arrived.

Papa patted his ample chin with a napkin. "Off to see my brothers eat their fish and fowl, are you?" he asked their retreating backs.

Maman shook her head at him with a little frown, so he turned his attention to a platter of cold turbot, its elaborate jellied glaze already melting in the heat. I shuddered. Fish of any kind was nasty enough, but cold jellied fish was disgusting. I wouldn't taste it, no matter what!

Charles, who was sitting on a cushion on a chair beside Maman, began to fidget. "Maman, I'm so hot!" he whimpered. His cheeks were flushed scarlet, and his silky hair hung in damp ringlets on his lace collar.

"Be patient, *chou d'amour*," soothed Maman. "You must be polite, you know, because all these nice people have come just to see us."

Obediently, Charles turned and smiled at the crowd, and was rewarded with approving murmurs. A few of the women blew kisses to him, and he delighted them by blowing one back.

Nice people, indeed! I thought. Nosey people, more like.

Maman, meanwhile, was smiling brightly, but I wasn't fooled. She hated these public occasions as much as I did. I was just more honest about it, that was all. Or to put it another way, Maman was very charming, whereas I have a face that shows exactly what I feel, and I'm very bad at pretending. Maman often called me *Mousseline-la-sérieuse*.

Catching my eye, she leaned toward me and whispered, "For heaven's sake, Mousseline, don't you stare at me too. And don't look so solemn. *Smile!*"

But I didn't want to smile at these people who stared at us so greedily. They said anything that came into their heads right out loud, too.

"*They* can afford enough bread," I heard a fellow with fierce moustaches mutter to his companion. She nodded, her eyes fixed on the golden loaves set out on the table.

Enough bread? I wondered. Surely everyone had plenty of that.

"Serious little thing, isn't she?" a fat man in the crowd remarked, staring hard at me.

"Haughty little thing, you mean." Someone snickered. "Like mother, like daughter. It's the Austrian pride, you know."

Bright colour rose in Maman's cheeks. I lowered my eyes to my plate. Why *Austrian* pride? It was true that Maman had been an Austrian archduchess before she married Papa, but that had been a long time ago. Yet I knew these people didn't like Maman. The feeling crackled in the air around us.

Fish, fowl, roast, game, another roast, savories, ices, compotes . . . Would the meal never end? Mercifully, the crowd finally began to thin out as people went to watch members of the family in other parts of the palace, or sought cooler air outdoors. At last Papa pushed back his chair and dinner was over. He rose, offering his arm to Maman. Yolande de Polignac collected Charles, and I fell in behind them with the other ladies.

There were cheers from the remaining spectators.

"Long live the King!"

"And the Dauphin!"

Only a few scattered voices added, "And the Queen."

Nodding to the crowd, Papa led the way back to the Queen's Chamber. There he left us to go back to his own rooms. The usual crowd of courtiers would be waiting for him. Everyone wanted something from the King of France. A pension, a place in the army, a place at court, a title of nobility, a grant of land, a favour for a friend – the list was endless. Sometimes it seemed as if the whole world came to Versailles, and hung about waiting.

Probably that's one of Papa's Sorrows, I thought.

Maman's temper had not improved with keeping. She sailed straight into her private suite, and once there she rounded on me. "What, exactly, do you think you're doing, Mousseline?" she snapped. "To show up tricked out in such a formal dress at midday! Madame de Mackau will hear of my displeasure, and so will Madame de Fréminville."

I dropped my eyes to avoid her angry gaze. It had been a big mistake. I could see that now.

"And that's not all," she went on. "You *must* make an effort to be agreeable when we dine in public. Nobody wants to see such a gloomy face. Charles puts you to shame!" Without waiting for a reply, she swept away into her *boudoir*.

Charles, grinning, was handed over to the people

of his houshold to be taken back to his chambers. He stuck his tongue out at me as he was led away.

I returned the compliment. Then I trudged back down the stairs to my own rooms, my ladies-in-waiting trailing behind me as hot and cross as two pea-hens. By now my beautiful gown was soaked under my arms with sweat, and its train draggled like a leaden tail behind me. I'd ruined it. And I had got Frémi in trouble. And Madame de Mackau would lecture me about my foolishness, and refuse to buy me another dress. At least, probably not one with *paniers*.

2

Passages

Early July, 1789

A quick glance over my shoulder to make sure no one was looking. Good! I pushed aside the tapestry and pressed one of the carved flowers on the wood panelling. With a tiny click a section of the panel sprang ajar, revealing a narrow flight of stairs. I scrambled through, pulling the secret door closed behind me. The gilded walls of Versailles were honeycombed with these back stairs and passages. Some led to the servants' quarters, others to small kitchens and service rooms located on floors above.

The little staircase was hot and stuffy. When I reached the top, I tiptoed along a narrow corridor and scratched lightly on a panel in the wall. After a moment, it opened, and my cousin Antoine d'Artois, the Duc d'Angoulême, pulled me through. His little black eyes and long nose had always reminded me of a monkey's. They still did, even though he was fifteen, almost grown up.

"You got my note," he said, grinning. "I thought it was time we had a game. We haven't played for nearly a year."

I grinned back. "About time we gave the grown-ups the slip."

We were in a small chamber off the staircase behind my mother's apartments. Antoine's younger brother Ferdinand was there, and so, to my horror, was Charles. He smirked at me, knowing very well that I wasn't glad to see him.

I scowled at the monkey. "You're mad, Antoine," I said. "It'll spoil everything to have Charles along. If they miss him they'll turn the palace upside down looking for him. Besides, he's the world's biggest tattletale. He'll be sure to tell Maman, and we'll never hear the end of it!"

Antoine shrugged. "What could I do?" he said. "He found out from Ferdinand and insisted he wanted to play. He threatened to tell if we wouldn't let him!"

"Oh, Charles," I sighed. "You are such a pest."

Charles stuck out his lower lip and glared up at me. "You never want me to play, Mousseline," he complained. "And it's better with more players."

"Yes, but you're such a baby. Last time you got scared and started to cry."

"That was last year. I'm much bigger now."

"And even more spoiled," I muttered.

"Let's get on with the game," said Antoine.

We trooped through the door in the panel. Antoine came last, and carefully closed it after us. At the top of the stairs he said, "All right. I'll be It, and start counting. Now, Charles and Ferdinand, you must promise not to go out into any of the public rooms to hide. There are plenty of closets and cupboards right in the passageways and service rooms. Agreed?"

They nodded. Antoine turned his back and started to count.

Stifling giggles, the little boys scurried away down the passage. I whisked around a corner and ran up another flight of stairs. At some times of the day, these passages were as busy as an ant heap, with servants rushing to attend the hundreds of lords and ladies who lived squeezed into the palace. Everything people needed to live passed this way – special meals, cleaned clothes and bed linens, chamber pots . . .

I sniffed and wrinkled my nose. Definitely chamber pots, and someone hadn't been too careful with one of them around here! But then, Versailles always stank of bad drains, and the hot summer only made it worse.

Where to hide? I spied a linen press at the far end of the passage. I was in luck. It had shelves on one side only, so there was just room for me to squeeze myself in, pack my skirts around me and pull the door shut. For once, being so short was an advantage rather than a Sorrow.

The sheets stacked on the shelves beside me smelled sweetly of orris root, but the closet was stiflingly hot. It must have been dusty too, because my nose began to prickle. And then – "Ah-CHOO!"

As I fished out my handkerchief, the door of the press was jerked open. I expected to see Antoine grinning at me, but it was only a plump chambermaid, her eyes as big as saucers beneath the frill of her cap. Dropping a quick curtsey, she seized an armload of sheets and slammed the door shut.

A fine tale she'd have to tell in the servants' hall tonight. Luckily for me, nobody who mattered would hear a word about it. Only servants came here, and any of them who saw us would simply pretend they hadn't. After all, if the lords and ladies of our own households couldn't mind us better, why should servants worry their heads about it?

By now I was smothering, though. Cautiously I inched the door open to let in a breath of fresher air.

And there was Antoine, waiting like a smug cat at a mousehole. "Caught you," he said, grinning, as he tagged me.

"Bother," I said, shaking the dust out of my skirts. "How'd you find me?"

"Well, for one thing, it was such an obvious place to hide that I knew you'd choose it!"

"Pooh," I said. "You've hidden in plenty of worse places!"

"And," he went on, "I met a flustered chambermaid with an armload of sheets. So I quickly deduced . . . "

"You and your deductions," I snapped. "I don't know why you bother playing with us, if it's all so simple. Why don't you just stick to your boring old chess?"

"Oh, come, Mousseline," he said. "Unruffle your feathers. You know I play once in a long while because the little fellows like it. And because I get to talk to you, instead of just bowing to you at mass."

I tossed my head. Antoine and I had been playmates when we were little, but he had pretty much ignored me for years now, saying I was too young to be any fun, and a girl into the bargain. But recently he had begun to seek me out and pay me compliments. I didn't like it much. I suspected his papa had put him up to it. Maman said that Oncle Charles would like it very much if Antoine and I got married some day. Too bad! If I got married at all, it would be to a great king in some foreign country, not to boring old Antoine.

"Also," Antoine went on, "one overhears some interesting things now and then in these passages. The servants always seem to know everything that's going on. Why shouldn't I pick up what I can?"

"Gossip," I said, trying to sound disdainful – though I've always been quite fond of gossip, if it's about people I know.

"Not just gossip," he replied. "Politics."

I groaned. "What could possibly be interesting about *that*?"

Antoine rolled his eyes. "You are *such* a featherbrain," he said. "Don't you ever think of anything besides your horse and your *paniers*?"

It was quite true that Marron, my pony, was the

light of my life. As for my fancy gowns, well, I now had one fewer of them.

"Come on," said Antoine, seizing my hand. "We must find the boys. Let's try the floor below."

We ran downstairs and started peering into closets and service rooms. In one room seamstresses were at work near a small window, mending ladies' dresses. Antoine stopped and put his finger to his lips, and we listened.

"Well, I'm finally done with Madame de Joinville's gown," said one, holding up a dress of richly brocaded silk. "Her maid has come here asking for it at least six times already today."

"From all the fuss she's making, you'd think Madame had only the one to wear," said another, tossing her head.

"No chance of that, is there? It's only the likes of us that have but one dress to our backs," said the first.

"*Mais oui*, and one dark little room to share."

"What, Claudine? And I always thought you lived in a palace of your own!" teased the oldest.

They all tittered. Then they noticed us standing in the doorway, and scrambled up, bobbing curtsies.

"Your pardon, mesdemoiselles," said Antoine. "Have you seen my brother, the Duc de Berry?"

There was something suspicious about the glances they exchanged.

My eye fell on a large wicker clothes hamper. Was it just my imagination, or had it jiggled a little? Advancing on the hamper, I flung back the lid and plunged both arms into the clothes, up to my elbows. Up popped Ferdinand like a plum out of a pudding.

The seamstresses giggled.

"Well," said Antoine as he closed the door behind us. "That leaves Charles."

But Charles was nowhere to be found. An hour passed, and I was getting worried. So was the monkey.

"We've gone and lost the future king of France," he groaned.

"I told you he'd spoil everything," I said. "Where can the little nuisance be?"

"There's the attics," Ferdinand piped up.

And that's where we found him, hidden in one of the winter stoves that were stored up there. We pulled him out, then stood gaping. For Louis Charles de Bourbon, Duc de Normandie and Dauphin de France, was covered in soot from head to foot, except for his cheeks, where tears had made strange white tracks down his face.

If Maman sees him like this, she'll die, I thought, horrified.

Charles blinked up at us. "Why didn't you come for so long?" he demanded.

"We couldn't find you, that's why!" I snapped.

His eyes lit up. "You mean I win?" he asked, beaming.

Antoine threw back his head and laughed. Trust the monkey to think it was funny.

I sighed. "Yes, Charles. You win." Somehow, he always did.

3

Clouds

July 15 – 17, 1789

One fine morning not long afterward, I woke up invisible. At least, I might as well have been invisible, because suddenly everyone seemed to look straight through me, as if I were made of glass. When Pompette, my little maid, drew back the bed curtains, her face was sticky with tears.

"Why, Pompette, what's the matter?" I asked sleepily.

Her eyes slid past me, and she turned away. Behind her stood Frémi, her face white and set.

I sat up. "Frémi, what is it?" Then, trying to make her smile, I said, "You must have had vinegar for breakfast."

No smile. She just took my chemise and petticoats from the wardrobe woman and held them out, gazing over the top of my head. "Your Highness must ask Madame de Mackau," she said distantly.

21

"*She* won't tell me anything, and you know it," I said, shrugging into my chemise. Then I flounced over to the basin Frémi held out and splashed my face with water, getting quite a lot of it on her gown too. "I'll go straight to Maman," I spluttered. I wouldn't really have dared, but I thought the threat might get something out of Frémi.

"You mustn't do that, Madame," she said hastily, handing me a towel. "Her Majesty must be . . . must be busy this morning."

I plunged through the bottom of the gown the wardrobe maid was holding, and emerged at the top. "Then *you* tell me," I grumbled. "I won't be ignored!"

But I was. With the macaw, it was the same story as with Frémi. She just looked through me. It was as if I suddenly didn't matter at all.

There was nothing to do though, except blunder through my morning lessons as usual. Then I ate dinner. Then I did more lessons, and practised the harpsichord. I *hate* the harpsichord. It sounds like a birdcage being plucked with a toasting fork.

At last Madame de Mackau carted me off to Charles's rooms. Strange – why did they want us to be together? I hardly ever went to his rooms, and he never came to mine. Some days I didn't even see him at all.

Ferdinand was there too. He and Charles were busy playing a game. Madame de Mackau sat me down to my embroidery. She always said that needlework soothed the nerves. Not mine. My thread got as tangled as my thoughts, and I had to unpick more than I sewed. At last I threw down the embroidery hoop and glared at the macaw. She didn't even notice.

Then gradually, I became aware of a sound in the distance. Cheering.

The macaw lifted her head, listening. Then the double doors swung open and one of Maman's ladies-in-waiting rushed in.

"Quick!" she gasped to Madame de Mackau. "Her Majesty wishes you to bring Their Highnesses to His Majesty's apartments – at once!"

The macaw whisked us upstairs and across the palace to Papa's rooms. There Maman scooped up Charles and Papa took me by the hand. Out we hurried onto a balcony that overlooked the courtyard. Below us, a huge crowd was cheering and tossing their hats in the air.

Nod, smile, bow, curtsey, wave. Then Maman told the macaw to take us back to Charles's rooms.

"What is it? Why are they cheering?" I kept asking as I was half-dragged along by the hand. Of course I got no answer.

Ferdinand was waiting for Charles, and the two of them were soon deep in their game again. I sat by myself, my head in a whirl. What strange kind of day was this? I had never known anything like it in my life!

Not long afterward, the door opened and Antoine came in.

Here was my chance to find out something! I jumped up.

He nodded politely to Madame de Mackau and gave Ferdinand a friendly cuff. Then he sauntered over to me.

"Well, at least *you* look me in the eye," I said loudly, meaning the macaw to hear.

The monkey winced. "You needn't bellow, Mousseline!"

I blushed. My voice isn't exactly musical, and when I get upset or excited, I sound like a crow. Another Sorrow.

"Come sit by the window," Antoine said in a low voice.

I nodded, smiling sweetly at him. A four-tooth smile, my very best. "What's going on? For pity's sake, tell me," I begged, pulling him down onto a sofa beside me. "I've been ignored all day, then dragged across the palace and back, and I *still* don't know what's happening!"

"There was a revolt in Paris yesterday," he said. "Mousseline, you won't believe it. The governor of the Bastille prison has been killed. His head was put on a pike and paraded through the streets! And the people of Paris have seized weapons from the government arsenal."

I thought he was making a bad joke. "Don't be silly, Antoine," I said. "Why would anyone want to revolt?"

Antoine stared at me, then rolled his eyes. "You really are a featherbrain! Haven't you paid attention to *anything* that's been going on all these months?" he asked "The crisis over taxes? The Estates-General? The new National Assembly?"

I tossed my head. "Why should I care about any of that?"

He started to say something, but I cut him off. "Oh, yes, I know. *You* care. And you've tried to talk to me about it. But it's all so boring." I wrinkled my nose. "This revolt surely can't be very dangerous to *us*. Why, the people cheered us not one hour ago!"

"We are safe enough – for the moment. But Oncle Louis has agreed to send away the army that protects Paris and Versailles. *That's* what all the cheering was about. There are still some loyal guards here, but . . . " Antoine shook his head. "Some people are going to have to flee France right away."

"Some people? Who?"

"Us. That is, Papa, and all the rest of my family. And your mother's friends Yolande and Louise."

"But *why*?" None of it made the least bit of sense to me. Why in the world should my uncle and his family have to leave France? As for my mother's friends, well, good riddance. Yolande de Polignac, Charles's governess, was a cat, with claws, and Louise de Lamballe was a goose. I had never understood why Maman liked them.

Antoine shrugged. "Because we're hated so much. At least, my papa is. You know how he loves to gamble. He loses huge sums at it. And he's always building himself fancy palaces. He's accused of squandering money while the people go hungry. Your maman's friends are too, they and their greedy relatives and all their titles and state pensions and land. Not to mention all the expensive gifts the Queen has given them. The people of Paris hate them as much as they do Papa. They've even put a price on their heads! If we stay, Oncle Louis's ministers tell him he may not be able to protect us."

What did Antoine mean? Oh, everyone complained about Oncle Charles's gambling and the gifts Maman gave her friends. I'd heard plenty of gossip about that. But what was this about the people going hungry? Papa wouldn't let his people starve!

They can afford enough bread . . .

For some reason the words of the man who had watched us dine popped into my head. But it was too ridiculous. Of course they had bread. Everybody did, didn't they? As for the other silly thing Antoine had said . . .

"My papa, the King of France, not able to protect his own brother? Don't be foolish, Antoine!" I snapped.

"It's true! Even the servants are whispering about it. They say this is more than a revolt," he insisted. "A lot of old scores are being settled. Grievances that go back hundreds of years. The people are tired of taxes and more taxes. A revolution, they're calling it. And even loyal troops don't always stay loyal!"

A long moment passed. I couldn't believe the monkey was serious, and we sat there staring at each other. "Well, then. When are you going?" I asked at last.

He took my hand, and rose to his feet, pulling me up with him. "Soon. Perhaps tomorrow." He bent over my hand and kissed it.

It tickled, and the thought of Antoine kissing any part of me made me want to giggle.

"Au revoir, Mousseline," he said. "Will you think of me sometimes?"

"Don't be silly, Antoine," I said. "I suppose I'll think of you. But you probably won't have to go after all."

Antoine shook his head. He crossed the room and put his hand on Ferdinand's shoulder. "Come along, Ferdi," he said. "Maman will be wanting us very soon."

Ferdinand opened his mouth to protest, but something in Antoine's face convinced him. He scrambled up and the two of them went out hand in hand. The footman swung the gilded door shut behind them.

Charles came over and tugged at my hand. "Antoine ruined our game," he complained. "Just when I was winning, too. You come play, Mousseline."

"Oh, all right, spoiled baby. I'll play with you," I said. But my thoughts were racing. What Antoine had said was impossible. But . . . revolution. There was something about that word. It sounded like thunder.

The next morning Antoine and his family were gone. So were my mother's friends. But the palace still echoed with the sounds of slamming doors and scurrying, hurrying footsteps. Trunks and boxes appeared out of nowhere – mountains of them were piled up in the corridors, then trundled down the staircases to waiting coaches. It seemed as if people were running away.

As for me, I was still invisible. It was time to act. I planted myself in front of the macaw, and glared up at her. "Madame, I won't do my lessons. Or read, or sew, or even eat," I growled. "Not until you tell me what's going on. Antoine told me all about the revolt, so you might as well tell me the rest of it."

As soon as the word "revolt" crossed my lips, I suddenly became visible again. My governess stared at me, then she nodded. "Paris is still up in arms. His Majesty may be going there tomorrow," she said.

Papa go to Paris? But he never went to Paris if he could help it. He always said Paris meant nothing but speeches and more speeches, something he hated.

"But the rebels, the revolution. Isn't it dangerous?" I whispered.

"His Majesty has his personal guards, Your Highness. He says it is his duty to try to calm the people." The macaw skewered me with a gaze as sharp as a gimlet, then added, "And if I may say so, it is your duty to be obedient and not cause problems for any of us during this difficult time."

Well! I opened my mouth and closed it again. "I'll . . . I'll try," I croaked.

The macaw's beady eyes softened a bit. "Good. Here is your German grammar book. Please go on with your lesson."

28

And so I did, and the day passed somehow. The next day Papa went to Paris. I heard a great bustle when he left, then settled down to wait for news – any news. Hours passed, and still more hours. At last, early in the evening, I was summoned to my mother's rooms. When I got there, I couldn't believe my eyes. The usual crowd of courtiers was nowhere to be seen. Half-packed travelling boxes stood about, and discarded clothing was strewn everywhere. Maman, pale and dishevelled, sat staring silently into the fireplace, which was choked with half-burned papers. Beside her in an armchair sat Charles, looking scared.

So Maman had asked for him first, not me.

The Princesse Élisabeth, Papa's younger sister, hurried forward and hugged me. Tante Babet was a tall woman, with rosy cheeks and masses of glossy chestnut hair. In my game I'd long ago decided that she was a hound – a noble, faithful hound.

"Poor Mousseline!" she exclaimed. "You should have been sent for before this, and not left to wonder and wait. But I've only just arrived at Versailles."

So it was she who had sent for me. Not Maman at all!

"Tante Babet, what's wrong with Maman?" I mumbled, my nose pressed into the ruffles on the front of her dress.

"She's terrified because your father hasn't returned from Paris. She believes he may have been taken prisoner. So she has been preparing to join him."

Papa a prisoner? But the people loved Papa! They

had cheered us all, hadn't they? Surely they wouldn't harm him.

I must have turned pale, because Tante Babet said quickly, "No, no, Mousseline, we have no reason to think that. Your mother just frets overmuch sometimes."

Well, that was true enough.

So we settled down to wait. Charles fell asleep curled up in the armchair. On Maman's mantel was a clock that chimed each quarter hour with a little tune: "It is raining, shepherdess. Gather in your sheep . . . " I had always loved its silvery sound, but now, as the leaden hours passed, I decided I hated it.

At last, late in the evening, horses clattered into the courtyard. Voices echoed, doors slammed, footsteps sounded on the stairs. In a few minutes my father tramped in, dusty and weary, but safe. My mother threw herself into his arms, while the rest of us clung about him.

As soon as we would let him, Papa dropped into a chair, tossing his plumed hat into another. Charles crawled sleepily onto his knees.

"May I never, never have to live another such day as that," Papa said. "Hours and hours just to reach Paris, because the crowds on the road were so dense. And when I finally got there, speeches and more speeches for hours. The people simply refused to part with me."

I picked up his hat and dusted it off with my handkerchief. There was a strange ribbon pinned to it, a red, white and blue cockade.

"What's this funny-looking thing, Papa?" I asked, holding it up.

"You're looking at the new national colours of France," he replied wearily. "The people of Paris have chosen them. No more royal lilies on white."

My mother's eyes blazed. Snatching the cockade from my hand, she threw it on the floor and trampled on it. "How could you let them subject you to that!" she raged. "Wear their colours, indeed! How can you bear such indignities?"

Papa shrugged. "It seemed necessary to calm them," he said.

In her sensible way, Tante Babet had ordered supper as soon as she heard Papa arrive. She knew how hungry he would be. Papa ate a roast chicken and four cutlets, and drank a little wine. Then he pushed his chair back and got clumsily to his feet, as Charles had fallen asleep on his lap.

"Now let me sleep for a thousand years!" he muttered as he put Charles into Maman's arms.

I plucked at his coat sleeve. "Papa?" I asked. There was so much I wanted to know, but I couldn't find the words.

"What is it, Mousseline?" he asked.

What did I hope he would say? That it was all some incredible mistake?

Papa put his big hand on my hair for a moment. "For now, all is well," he said. "But when you say your prayers, my child, pray for France."

The door closed behind him. I listened as his heavy footsteps died away down the corridor. It was the loneliest sound in the world.

4

Strangers

August 1789

At first I woke up each morning wondering what strange and awful thing would happen next. But after several weeks passed, I began to think things couldn't have been nearly as bad as the grown-ups had feared.

Some of the courtiers trickled back to Versailles, looking shamefaced at having scampered off so rudely. And life went on as before – almost. There were no more entertainments or receptions, and we didn't dine in public anymore. We only appeared in public to go to mass.

Papa was meeting day after day with the National Assembly or with his ministers, and we hardly ever saw him. When I asked the macaw why he was so busy, she just said, "Those hotheads in Paris have settled down, thank Heaven. But now the members of the Assembly are talking a great deal of foolishness. His Majesty is attempting to reason with them."

Whenever Papa could steal some time from politics, though, I knew he still tramped up to the attic where he kept his forge and anvil. His great hobby was locksmithing, and he used to say that working with his hands helped him think. I guessed that he must be doing a lot of that now.

In the past he used to emerge, grimy-handed, to show us the latest complicated mechanism he had made. Maman had never cared for this. "Such a common habit," I'd heard her complain to Tante Babet.

Tante Babet had smiled and shrugged. "Now, Antoinette, you know very well that nobody thought Louis would ever be king. That's why he was allowed a modern education and learned manual arts."

"I know. But locksmithing?" Maman had wrinkled up her nose.

My aunt just laughed. "Consider yourself lucky. Louis learned to plough, too, but fortunately he didn't take to that!"

Poor Papa. Everyone knew that he hadn't really wanted to be king, but when his elder brother died he had to become heir to the throne. I didn't see why being king should stop him from doing something he liked to do.

As for Maman, she spent more time in her private rooms than she used to do, but she too had her escape. Her hobby was a miniature farm called the Hameau. It was located in a far corner of the palace grounds, and had a duck pond and a dairy and two enchanting goats called Blanchette and Brunette. I loved to walk about there, but Maman always preferred to go with just one or two close friends. Now she spent hours alone there, or in the gardens at Trianon she loved so well.

It was all very dull. I had no hobbies, and nothing to do but lessons. Sometimes I was allowed to go riding on Marron, but not nearly often enough. Still, everything seemed so quiet that little by little I stopped thinking about what had happened in July. Sometimes, though, I missed Antoine and wondered why he and his family hadn't come back. I decided that Oncle Charles must have found better places for gambling and horse racing. There was no sign of Maman's old friends Yolande and Louise, either. I suppose she must have missed them a lot. I didn't.

One afternoon in August, Maman sent for me. I found her in her Reception Chamber. Her ladies-in-waiting had been ordered to the far end of the room, and Maman was speaking with a woman I had never seen before. The lady was very tall, with grey hair and striking dark eyes. A noble deer, I decided. As she and Maman spoke, they kept glancing at Charles, who was leaning against Maman's chair, his big blue eyes fixed on the stranger.

"Thérèse," said Maman, turning to me, "this is the Duchesse de Tourzel. Madame de Tourzel, my daughter, Marie Thérèse Charlotte, Madame Royale."

This last was my official title. It meant that I was the eldest daughter of the king and queen of France, and people at court usually called me "Madame" or "Your Highness," not "Princesse." Nobody *ever* called me "Mademoiselle." That would have been much too informal – even *I* knew enough about etiquette to know that!

The Duchess curtsied, smiling.

"Madame de Tourzel will be superintending both your and Charles's households now," said Maman. She turned back to the Duchess. "As you know, these duties belonged before to my dear friend Yolande de Polignac."

"I'm sure she is greatly missed," said Madame de Tourzel discreetly.

Something in the set of her mouth told me she had no great opinion of Yolande. I felt myself warming to this woman. She didn't flutter or act nervous, as so many people did around my family.

"And, Thérèse," Maman was saying, "this is Pauline, Madame de Tourzel's youngest daughter. From now on, Pauline will live here at Versailles with us. I'm sure the two of you will soon become the best of friends."

"Your Royal Highness," the girl murmured, making a very neat curtsey. Not a wobble in sight.

Until then I had paid no attention to her. Now I looked her over thoroughly. She looked older than I was, a little. Had dark eyes like her mother's. Was slender, and pretty – and tall. Why did she have to be tall?

Gazelle, I thought.

She blushed, almost as if she had read my thoughts.

Then Charles drew himself up to his small height and said, "Maman forgot to introduce me properly, Mademoiselle. I'm Louis Charles, Duc de Normandie. I'm Dauphin now, but someday I'll be King, after Papa."

Pauline's eyes danced. "I'm honoured to make your acquaintance too, Your Royal Highness," she said demurely, dropping another curtsey.

"I think you can see what you'll be dealing with, Madame," said my mother, turning back to the Duchess with an indulgent smile. "Charles will require most of your care, no doubt. Thérèse, being older, will require only general supervision. Madame de Mackau oversees her immediate needs." She rose, ending the interview.

Madame de Tourzel curtsied deeply. "I understand, Your Majesty. I'll do everything in my power to deserve your confidence." Then she held out her hand to Charles and said, smiling, "Come with me, my little prince."

To my surprise, my willful little brother obeyed at once, only turning back to ask, "Is Pauline coming too?"

"Yes, I am, Your Highness."

The door closed behind the three of them. I stood looking at it, feeling left out.

❧ ❧ ❧

Maman's prediction about Pauline and me didn't come true. We didn't become friends. Why should we? After all, you can put two cats in a bag, but that doesn't mean they'll agree. The truth was, Pauline was another Sorrow. She and I had to spend almost every hour of every day together, and I soon found out that she was far ahead of me in almost every subject. German, Latin, French composition – all came easily to her. The Abbé Morin, my tutor, made a huge fuss about how clever she was. And she was accomplished too. The dancing master was delighted with her gracefulness, and even my grumpy old macaw praised her music and needlework. Of course, all this was reported to Maman. *She* also began praising Pauline, at least when I was in the room.

As for Pauline, she worshipped Maman, and was always saying how charming she was.

I wasn't charming. No danger of that. All this "Paulinery" put me out of countenance. Nobody understood how I felt. Nobody cared. I thought Tante Babet at least would sympathize, but even she laughed at me.

"Poor Mousseline. Now you're paying for all your laziness. No, don't scowl at me, child," she added. "I used to be exactly like you. I drove all my tutors and governesses to despair too."

Sometimes I felt so cross that it took a long hard gallop on Marron to get rid of my sulks.

Pauline understood perfectly how I felt about her. When the two of us were together, she was polite, but watchful. *En garde*, Mademoiselle, I thought to myself. You don't like me any better than I like you.

Of course, Charles adored Pauline just as everyone else did. Sometimes I'd see the two of them tossing a ball or playing backgammon, and Pauline would look like a different person, her face flushed and her eyes lit with laughter. What a change from the prim creature I spent my days with.

One morning I came upon them sitting cozily together. Charles's curly fair head and Pauline's smooth dark one were bent over a book of fairy tales. Pauline was reading aloud, while Charles leaned against her shoulder looking at the pictures.

I felt . . . I don't know what I felt. "I'd like to speak to my brother, Mademoiselle. Privately," I snapped. As Pauline shut the book and stood up hastily, I added, "And in future please remember that it isn't your job to entertain him. I don't know what you're used to at home, but here at Versailles there are plenty of nursemaids for that."

Pauline flushed, but said only, "I understand, Madame." She curtsied and left the room.

"Oh, Mousseline, you *are* nasty," Charles pouted. Picking up the book, he trotted over to the door. "I'm going right after her to tell her how much I like the way she reads to me. She's much better than any nursemaid. And she's *much* nicer than you!"

Sudden tears stung my eyes. I'd never bothered to wonder what Charles thought of me. I tried to make excuses to myself. It's not fair . . . I only meant . . . Then I got angry. As if it mattered whether either of them liked me! Why should I care?

5

Thunder

October 6, 1789

One wild, wet day I was kneeling on the window seat in my chamber, my nose squashed against the pane, watching low clouds scudding above the trees of the palace park. Pauline and I had done lessons all morning, and I had suffered away at the harpsichord. We had been promised a drive afterwards, but now the bad weather meant there was nothing to do until dinnertime. Something about the weather made me feel wild. I could have bitten somebody.

Pauline, needless to say, was stitching quietly away at her embroidery.

Madame de Mackau suggested that I might like to do the same. "Are you not embroidering a vest for His Majesty? Might he not be expecting to wear it someday soon?" she asked.

"Indeed, and he shall have it, Madame. If he and I both live long enough." I made a face. "Anyway, I'd far rather be out hunting, like Papa. Better to be soaking wet and caked with mud than have nothing to do but boring lessons and stupid embroidery!"

The macaw sniffed expressively.

The Duchess and Charles joined us at dinnertime. Just as we were finishing, we heard rapid footsteps in the passage. Then Tante Babet burst into the room. Her riding habit was splashed with mud, and her hair was wet and windblown, as if she had ridden without a hat.

We gaped at her. Princesses were never, ever supposed to look like this!

"Madame de Tourzel, where is the King?" she demanded.

No courteous nod of the head. No polite tone of voice.

Well! No etiquette today!

"Why, His Majesty is hunting, Your Highness. At Meudon," replied the Duchess.

"And the Queen?"

"At Trianon, since this morning."

"A word with you, Madame," my aunt said, beckoning. The two of them went out into the corridor, and the door clicked shut behind them. I would have loved to tiptoe over and put my ear against it, but didn't quite dare to.

It was well that I didn't, because after only a moment, Madame de Tourzel returned alone. She looked rather shaken.

What could Tante Babet have said to stir up the Duchess like that?

"If Your Highness is finished," Madame de Tourzel said to me, "let's go to Monsieur le Dauphin's rooms. Her Majesty has been sent for, and that's where she will expect to find us. Something has happened. I will say no more for now." Dismissing the macaw with a nod, she took Charles by the hand and led the way from the dining room.

It was almost an hour before Maman appeared, anxious and pale.

Something really tremendous was going on. But what?

"Where is the King?" Maman asked urgently.

"Not yet returned, Your Majesty," said the Duchess. "Though messengers were sent after him some time ago."

Maman kissed Charles and hurried away. Madame de Tourzel took him on her knee and began to read him a story.

"*Someone* should tell me what's happening," I growled.

The Duchess gave me what I had come to know as The Look – a steady, wondering gaze, as if she couldn't believe what she was hearing. She went on with the story. Not until it was finished and Charles had been handed over to a nursemaid for his nap did she turn to me.

"Madame," I said, "I – "

"You needn't tell me, Your Highness," she said, with her cool smile. "It's written all over you. You're dying of curiosity about what's going on."

To my surprise, Pauline spoke up. I wouldn't have thought she had it in her.

"Don't you think it's worse for us not knowing, Maman?" she asked.

The Duchess looked at us keenly. Then she shrugged. "I think it can't do any harm to tell you what I know," she said. "It's little enough. The Princesse Élisabeth heard this morning that a large crowd of rioters is marching to Versailles from Paris. She even saw some of them on the road herself, and rode cross country to warn us. It's said they're coming to demand something from His Majesty or the Assembly." She got up, putting the book aside.

From Papa? What could they want? And what if the crowd reached Versailles before Papa got back? What if he couldn't win through? But surely he would. And then . . . and then he'd know what to do.

"Don't worry. I'm sure His Majesty will be back soon," said the Duchess. "Meanwhile, my place is with the Dauphin." She went out, closing the door behind her.

Of course her place was with the Dauphin. Because if anything happened to my father, my little brother would be King of France.

Feeling rather sick, I went over to the window and leaned my forehead against the cold glass. After awhile, I realized Pauline was standing behind me.

I was so miserable I had to talk to someone, even The Perfect One. "It's beginning again," I said. "You weren't here back in July, you don't know how awful

43

it was. People ran away. Versailles was like a tomb for days, and we were buried alive in it. And Papa had to go to Paris, and we were so afraid. Then everything seemed all right again. But now . . ."

Pauline sighed. "Well, you won't have to worry about our deserting you," she said. "No matter what. You know my mother a little by now. She never runs away from anything."

She sounded so rueful. How she must be wishing she was anywhere but Versailles. Well, too bad for her.

"But what's wrong *now*?" I asked. "I thought the revolt, or revolution, or whatever it was, was over."

Pauline was silent. I knew she didn't want to talk to me. I could feel it.

At last she said, "I can tell you a little, if you really want me to."

I whirled around. "You? What can *you* possibly know about any of it?" I asked. I expected her to drop her eyes, or turn away. But she didn't.

"We lived on our country estate before we came here," she said. "With such a terrible drought this year, the harvest is poor." She hesitated, then went on. "The flour from last year is almost gone, you see, and there's not much flour yet from this year's harvest. That means there's not enough bread. Many people are going hungry, or can't afford the higher prices, and they . . . they blame the King."

They can afford enough bread, that man had said back in July, eyeing our golden loaves. Now it was beginning to make sense. But why blame Papa? "Why, Papa's the best of kings!" I protested.

"I only tell you what I've seen and heard for myself," said Pauline. "And there's worse. You seem to think the revolt ended in July. Well, it didn't. Oh, things quieted down in Paris. But in the countryside the peasants have been burning the châteaux of nobles like us down around our ears!"

"Burning down the châteaux?" Now I was bewildered. "But why would the peasants do that?"

"Well, for one thing they hate us because we are rich and they are poor. And because they don't have enough bread, and have to pay so many taxes. They burn down the châteaux to destroy the tax records. If there are no records, they don't have to pay the taxes, you see. So far my family's estate has escaped, but that's why my mother insisted I come with her when she was summoned to Versailles."

I was struck dumb. All this had been going on these weeks and I didn't know about it. It was like . . . like being kept in a cage. A cage of silence. For a moment I was angry. But I couldn't stay that way long – my thoughts were in too much of a whirl. I remembered what Antoine had said about my mother's friends, how Maman had showered them and all their relatives with money and gifts and titles and land. And this while the people were actually going hungry? Well, now those fine friends of hers were safely out of France and a mob was on its way to Versailles!

Darkness came early. Around five o'clock we heard

the clatter of hooves, then shouted commands from the courtyard. The palace echoed with the creaking of hinges, as gates that had stood open for uncounted years boomed shut.

Moments later Madame de Tourzel appeared. "His Majesty has returned safely, Madame," she said to me. Then, turning to Pauline, "It would be well, my daughter, if you tell your maid to pack some things for you. It may be that Their Majesties will decide to move farther away from Paris until these troubles subside."

Pauline hurried out, but returned in a few minutes, her eyes enormous. "They're at the gates," she said in a frightened voice. "Rioters!"

"Will we be leaving now?" I asked.

Pauline dropped her eyes. "I think it's too late! I heard a footman shout that the crowd has control of the stables and has surrounded the palace."

I peered out into the darkness. I could see torches winking like demon eyes out in the park.

After supper the Duchess took Charles and me upstairs to Maman. We all settled down to wait, and once again the silly tune of the clock chimed away the hours. Charles fell asleep, but I stayed awake, listening to the wind raging around the palace, rattling the shutters and driving rain against the windows. Sometimes I heard shouts and gunfire through the storm. What was happening? I strained my ears, but the voices were too far away to make out.

At last my father appeared. With him was General

Lafayette, the leader of the National Guard. A sleek, handsome man in a very fancy uniform, he bowed gallantly over my mother's hand. From the look on her face she didn't enjoy the attention much, and she took her hand away as soon as she could.

White rat, I thought. It was easy to see that the general considered himself the hero of the hour. He puffed out his chest, and his eyes roamed busily over us all, as if looking for the best way to turn us to his advantage. If he'd had whiskers, they would have been twitching.

"I have received a delegation from the crowd," Papa told Maman, "and promised to do everything I can to help them, even to give them all the bread and flour from our own kitchens. General Lafayette's men have the situation under control now, and are standing watch over the palace."

Maman turned to Madame de Tourzel. "The children may go to their rooms now. But remember, if anything happens, take Charles directly to His Majesty's apartments. Whatever you do, don't take him to mine!"

For a moment I didn't understand why. Then I did, and my heart sank. Maman knew how much the people hated her. If anything went wrong, she'd be in much greater danger than Papa. That's why Charles had to be taken to Papa's rooms if anything happened.

Madame de Tourzel carried Charles away, and Maman turned to kiss me goodnight. She was so distracted that she missed my forehead and kissed the air above me. "Try to sleep, Mousseline, and don't be afraid," she said. "The soldiers will protect us."

It was hard to obey. It was all very well for Maman to say we would be safe, but I wondered if she really believed it. I lay awake for a long time, listening, but could hear only the sound of the storm. At last I decided Maman had been right after all. Worn out with waiting and wondering, I fell asleep to the sound of the wind moaning in the chimneys.

6

Storm

October 7, 1789

I awoke with a start and held my breath, listening. The wind had died down and it was still pitch dark outside. Cries and shouts were coming from somewhere within the palace. I sat bolt upright, clutching the bedclothes. Suddenly I heard shots, screams and the sound of splintering wood and smashing glass right overhead. The rioters must be in Maman's rooms! What was happening to her?

I jumped out of bed and pulled a robe on over my nightgown. Then I wrapped myself in a blanket and stood trembling in the dark. Minutes passed, minutes that seemed like hours. What should I do? Would someone come for me? Had I been forgotten?

Then I heard heavy footsteps and the door burst open, letting a faint light spill into the room. My heart almost stopped as the figure of a man came toward me. But it was only Hanet, one of my footmen.

Without a word he scooped me up, blanket and all, and carried me up the back staircase that led to the floor above. As we neared the top I held my breath. The sounds coming through the walls from my mother's rooms were horrifying.

At the top Hanet carried me into a side passage. Then he put me down and we ran hand-in-hand toward Papa's apartments at the centre of the palace. Halfway there, Maman came running toward us. Barefoot, her hair loose upon her shoulders, she was wearing only a wrapper over her nightgown, and was clutching her stockings in one hand.

She hadn't forgotten me after all!

"Mousseline! Thank God you're safe," she cried.

"Maman! I was so frightened," I sobbed, flinging my arms around her. "I heard such dreadful sounds from your rooms. Screaming . . ."

"I know," Maman gasped, as we hurried on. "I was warned in time, and escaped before the rioters reached me. But two of my guards, they . . . they died to save me." She shuddered, and her eyes filled with tears. "Poor young men. They were killed defending my door against the mob. Without them I'd be dead now."

When we reached Papa's rooms I rubbed my eyes in disbelief. Half-burnt stubs of candles had been stuck hastily into all sorts of jars and dishes, and their fitful light set weird shadows dancing upon the walls. Above, the high ceilings loomed over us, lost in darkness. Strangest of all, people were in their nightclothes. The livid light made them look like ghosts and ghouls. I choked back a nervous hiccup of laughter at the sight of my crotchety great-aunts sitting bolt upright on a sofa, scowling at everyone – still wearing their nightcaps!

Outside the long windows, the darkness was red with the glow of thousands of smouldering torches. In my ears was a sound so fierce, so strange, that the hair stood up on the back of my neck. It was like the baying of wild animals, pierced by screams and the firing of muskets.

Papa was standing in the centre of the room, in a crowd of government ministers who were all speaking to him at once. The white rat general stood beside him, scowling, beating an impatient tattoo with his fist on the pommel of his sword. I noticed that he was the only one of us who was dressed properly. Every medal, every satin ribbon was in place on his perfect uniform.

Maman rushed over to where Madame de Tourzel stood holding Charles, and I followed. Maman took my brother in her arms, burying her face in his silky curls as if to blot out the world. "My poor baby," she murmured.

"How did the rioters get in?" I asked the Duchess.

She looked grim. "No one knows. Perhaps one of the guards was careless. And there was treachery. Someone led the rioters straight to Her Majesty's apartments. It's a miracle she escaped."

I shuddered. "And Pauline? Is she safe?" I asked.

Madame de Tourzel nodded. "She's in her room. The troops kept the rioters from that wing of the palace."

Meanwhile Charles was beginning to fret. "I'm hungry, Maman," he complained. "When will we have breakfast?"

"Be patient, *chou d'amour*. We can't think of that now."

Frustrated, Charles reached out and wound his fingers in my hair, giving it a sharp tug.

"Ow! Stop it, Charles!" But my protest was half-hearted. How I wished I were like him – too little to be afraid.

Other members of our family came running from their rooms in distant parts of the palace. The Comte de Provence, Papa's younger brother, hurried in with his powdered wig all frowsty and askew, and again I choked back nervous laughter. Last of all, Tante Babet appeared. She leaned against the doorway for a moment, quite out of breath. Everyone stared at her in horror, for her slippers and the hem of her white nightgown were drenched with blood!

"Babet! Where have you come from?" cried Maman.

Tante Babet hurried over and hugged her. "When I realized what was happening I tried to get to you," she gasped. "So I ran up the main stairs. The troops had got rid of the rioters, but there was blood, oh, everywhere! The bodies of your guards – *mon dieu*, they were headless! I was sure you were dead, An-

52

toinette." She embraced Maman again, her eyes brimming with tears.

I pressed myself close against her.

Outside, the howls and shrieks of the mob grew louder.

"What is it? What do they want?" I cried.

"I fear . . . they want the King." Tante Babet spoke calmly, but my arm was around her waist, and I could feel her trembling.

There was a rattle of musket shots like hail around the windows, and then, with one dreadful voice, the crowd began to chant. "The King! The King! The King to the balcony!"

Maman forced her way through the group around Papa and clung to him. "No, Louis. You mustn't! Those muskets . . . they mean to shoot you!"

General Lafayette frowned. "You must appear, Sire," he said. "If you don't, they may attack the palace again."

"If that happens, can you and your troops guarantee our safety?" Papa asked.

The general flushed. "The National Guard is newly formed, Your Majesty. Some of the troops are scarcely trained, and many have sympathy for the people."

"In other words, they are not to be trusted," said Papa heavily. "Very well. I must do anything necessary to protect my family."

"No!" cried Maman.

Tante Babet put her hand on my mother's arm. "It may . . . it may calm them, Antoinette," she said in a low voice. "Louis is well-loved despite these troubles, and the person of the king is still deeply respected."

Maman shook off her hand. "How can you encourage him to do something so dangerous? How *can* you?" she demanded.

But Papa had already nodded to the footmen, who stepped forward and swung the tall doors open onto the balcony. The roar of the crowd broke over us like a wave.

I pressed my hands over my ears and struggled to keep down a scream that was rising at the back of my throat. They were going to shoot Papa!

My father stepped forward onto the balcony, his heavy figure unmistakable even by torchlight.

"The King!" howled the mob in triumph. More muskets went off and I held my breath. Papa just stood there, solid as a rock.

Somehow, his courage must have touched them. One by one, then several, then many, voices began to chant, "Long Live the King! Long Live the King!"

They still loved Papa, then, even when they were so angry. They weren't going to kill him after all. Relief sent tears streaming down my cheeks.

Then the chant changed. "The King to Paris!" the mob clamoured.

After several minutes Papa stepped back into the room, pale but calm.

Then a new cry arose from below. "The Queen! The Queen! The Queen to the balcony!" Shrieks and wild laughter accompanied the chanting.

My mother shrank back.

"Madame, I think you must do it," urged General Lafayette.

"Maman, no!" I cried. They had no love for her the way they did for Papa. They would kill her!

Maman took a deep breath, then said, "Very well." She reached out a hand to Charles and to me. She meant us to go with her! I hung back a moment, then, trembling, I looked up at her and took her hand. Her face was set like a mask, and her hand was as cold as death.

She led us out into the awful vortex of sound on the balcony. I was so frozen with fear that I couldn't feel the floor under my feet, and stumbled as we walked toward the gilded railing of the balcony. There we stopped and looked down into the Marble Court below.

What a horrible change from the cheering crowd of last July! Now the courtyard was packed with wild-looking figures brandishing pikes, axes and smouldering torches. Some of them were waving muskets and firing them into the air.

Wolves! I thought, shivering.

When they caught sight of us, an eerie silence fell.

I gazed down, terrified. Then, out of the hundreds, maybe thousands of faces, my eyes fixed on a woman standing just below us. She was meagrely clothed, and in her arms she held a small child, not much younger than Charles. The child's eyes, wide with fear, gazed up at me as if I were a being from another world. Both mother and child were so pitiful, so thin! I had never imagined that people could be so poor, so hungry-looking. How could it happen? What could my father do for them?

My eyes locked with the woman's for a moment. And then she smiled, not mockingly, but kindly. Was *she* pitying *me?*

After a long moment, jeers, hisses and boos exploded into the air around us, and I cringed.

"No! The Queen alone! No children!" screamed a hoarse voice. The rest of the crowd took up the chant. "The Queen alone! The Queen alone!"

The woman with the child, though, she didn't chant. She just stared up at us, smiling still.

Maman dropped our hands. "Go back," she commanded. *"Vite!"* Charles and I shrank back inside the room. The Duchess caught Charles up, and Tante Babet put her arms around me.

Now Maman faced the mob alone, her hands crossed on her breast.

There was another moment of dreadful silence. Then, incredibly, a lone voice sang out, "Long Live the Queen!" A few scattered voices echoed the cry.

Maman sank into a graceful curtsey.

But now a new chant drowned out the cheers. "To Paris! The King and Queen to Paris!"

Maman stepped back through the doors, pale and trembling, and Charles and I threw ourselves on her.

Meanwhile, the general and Papa's minsters were insisting that we must leave Versailles and go to Paris as the people wished. Otherwise there would be even more violence.

At last my father made up his mind. Slowly, as if the words broke his heart, he said, "If there is no other way to avoid further bloodshed, we must go."

🌿 🌿 🌿

In just a few hours it was time to leave. Dressed in my plainest gown and mantle, I looked about my room one last time. It was a beautiful morning now, and the sun gleamed on the dainty gilded woodwork and embroidered hangings. Would I ever see this room again? Or would a mob break into it to hack and destroy as they had done in my mother's rooms?

A little after one o'clock, we went down a back stairway to the courtyard where a line of carriages and wagons was drawn up. The crowd was waiting. Once again that awful roar broke over us, and I shrank back against Tante Babet.

"Courage, Mousseline," she murmured in my ear. "Try not to let them see that you're afraid."

Somehow our family all squeezed into one carriage. As it crept forward, the crowd swirled around us, screaming and brandishing ghastly trophies – the heads of my mother's slaughtered guards impaled on pikes. I buried my face in Tante Babet's shoulder.

"We are bringing to Paris the baker, the baker's wife, and the baker's boy," the mob chanted gleefully.

"What do they mean, Tante Babet?" I asked.

"They believe that your father can give them all

bread, that if he is in Paris the flour shortage will be over."

I thought of the half-starved mother and child in the courtyard. "But . . . but *can* Papa end the flour shortage?"

"Unfortunately, no."

Slowed by the crowd, our carriage moved no faster than a snail's pace. We didn't reach the gates of Paris until six in the evening. I listened numbly as the mayor made a very long speech. I was too tired to decide what animal he was. Not a very nice one. Then we rolled on through the narrow streets of the city. Crowds lined the way to gape at us. Cries of "Long Live the Nation!" rang in our ears.

It was ten o'clock before we reached the Tuileries. The old palace had stood dark and abandoned for fifty years, and nothing was ready for us. Crossing the threshold into the dark entrance hall, my mother suddenly burst into tears.

"Are you ill, Antoinette?" asked Tante Babet.

Maman shivered. "I am so cold, so cold. It's as if I had entered a tomb," she murmured.

Charles, waking up in Madame de Tourzel's arms, gazed in wonder at the cracked walls and dingy passageways. "It is all very ugly here, Maman," he pronounced solemnly. "I don't like it!"

My mother wiped her tears and tried to smile at him. "My child, your great ancestor Louis XIV lived here and liked it well enough. We mustn't be harder to please than he was," she said.

I didn't see how he could possibly have liked it, ever. Nobody could.

Somehow, beds were found for all of us. Pauline and some of Maman's ladies-in-waiting had to make do with sofas in a smelly old parlour. The room next door where Charles and I would sleep wasn't much better. Madame de Tourzel looked around it in disgust.

"It's disgraceful!" she burst out. "No guards. And the doors are so warped from damp that they can't be closed!" Furiously, she began tugging a heavy chest to barricade the doors. Footmen scurried to help her. Then she pulled up a chair and sat down bolt upright in front of it, guarding our door in person.

Thank heaven for the Duchess! I thought, a little comforted, as I drifted into sleep.

7

Letters

November 1789

I put down my pen and blew on my fingers to warm them. Winter was upon us, and the Tuileries was fearfully cold. Icy draughts gusted down the corridors and whined under the ill-hung doors, making the candles gutter and go out. Even worse was the damp.

I stretched out my hands to the small tiled stove that gave off a feeble warmth. "Wretched Tuileries," I grumbled. "No wonder Great-great-great-great-grandfather built himself another palace at Versailles. This one is horrid."

Louise de Lamballe, who was sitting across from me, tossed her blond curls and laughed. For Louise was back. Like most of Maman's fancy friends, she had fled France in July. But unlike all the rest, she hurried back to share our captivity the moment she heard we were shut up in the Tuileries. That took courage, I had to admit. Louise wasn't all bad, but that silvery laugh of hers got on my nerves.

"Well, it *is* horrid," I said, glaring at her. "It's run-down and shabby and cold. I've got so many clothes on I look like a bolster, and I'm still freezing."

Madame de Tourzel glanced up from the lesson she was giving Charles, and gave me The Look.

I bit my tongue.

Madame de Tourzel and Pauline now spent the whole day with us, too, so I got to hear more than ever about how perfect Pauline was. Maman was always casting her up to me – it was a little way she had of trying to improve me. Of course, Pauline was devoted to Maman, and Maman was always most fond of those who loved her best. I did try to please Maman, I really did. But it was as if nothing about me was right, ever.

One particularly cold day I'd said, "I wish Papa would hurry up and give the people what they want. Then we could all go home to Versailles."

For once, Maman's iron-clad etiquette had snapped. She rounded on me, her eyes as hard as blue pebbles. "Stupid child! Don't dare to criticize your papa and talk about things you don't understand!"

There I'd sat, embarrassed in front of them all. It wasn't fair. I wasn't really criticizing Papa – or anyone. I was just trying to understand. If it was just bread the people wanted, why couldn't we go home now? After all, the people now had all the bread from Versailles. I wouldn't mind going without bread, if only we could go home.

And of course I hadn't meant anything wrong

about Papa. I loved Papa more than anybody else. *He* never criticized me, and I knew he was as miserable at being locked up here as I was. He was used to going hunting every day, and now that he couldn't he got fatter and fatter. The only pleasure he had left was his locksmithing. He'd had his anvil and forge brought from Versailles, and at odd times of the day and night, he and his favorite locksmith would bang away. You could hear it all over the palace. It made Maman cross.

As I sat there brooding about my Sorrows, a mouse scuttled out from behind one of the draperies and made a dash for a hole in the wainscotting. Louise sprang from her chair with a cry, her handkerchief pressed to her lips. "Oh, did you see?" she faltered. "It was a, it was a . . . "

"Mouse," finished the Duchess, matter-of-factly.

"Or possibly a rat," added my mother, looking up with a smile from a letter she was writing.

"*Rat!*" Louise swayed on her feet and clung to the back of her chair. "I'm going to faint!"

Not again, I thought. Even Maman rolled her eyes. Louise was given to fainting fits on all occasions.

The Duchess, ever practical, got up and waved a bottle of ferocious-smelling salts under Louise's nose. Louise took a sniff, gasped and sneezed.

"After all, it was only a very *small* rat – I mean, mouse, Louise," teased Maman. "Don't you know that the Tuileries swarms with them? Why, they run all over the beds at night, and you have to bribe them with cheese to keep them from eating your dinner right off your plate!"

Louise raised a pale face from her handkerchief. "Oh, pray, don't joke, Your Majesty," she quavered. "You don't really mean that, do you?"

"Louise, you must know by now that Her Majesty is a terrible tease," said the Duchess.

Still smiling wickedly, Maman shrugged and picked up her letter. "Welladay, Duchess, you are right. I fear I am a very cruel woman. Louise, my dear, I promise that from now on the words r—— and m—— will never cross my lips in your hearing."

Sometimes I wished Maman would tease me in that charming way she had. If only I could find a way to make her pleased with me. Maybe then she would love me better. I sighed and I sank my chin onto my hands. How I longed for a gallop on Marron to get rid of all the cobwebs in my head. Or at least for a visit to Versailles so that I could be sure he was well taken care of. No matter how often I asked, I could never learn anything about him. People just thought animals didn't matter.

If only I had someone my own age to talk to! Someone other than Pauline, of course. Who could be friends with a Sorrow?

Just watching her sit there put me out of countenance. She was always embroidering, or reading, or playing with Charles, or writing letters to her friends. She got lots of letters – reams of them. I never did. Who would write to me, after all? Well, maybe Antoine. But even if he had written, the revolutionaries probably wouldn't have let me receive his letters.

Seeing Pauline getting all those letters began to bother me. I noticed she always went off into a corner to read them – just in case someone might ask her to share one, I guessed. So one day when I came upon her reading one, and no one else was around, I leaned over and snatched it right out of her hands.

The look on her face was a sight to see!

"It's all right," I said. "I'm just curious to see what all these friends of yours write to you about."

"But it's from my friend Sophie. It's private!" Pauline protested, stretching out her hand for the letter.

I held it just out of reach, and waved it back and forth. "So?" I asked. Ignoring her pleading look, I glanced down the page. I didn't really intend to read it. Or not much of it. But when my eye caught the words "King" and "Queen" I couldn't help but read on.

My dear Pauline, the letter began:

I can't tell you how sorry we all are to hear of your sad experiences in October, and also that your mother says you must continue where you are, with the King and Queen, instead of returning to be near us in the country. My dear Papa looked very grave when he heard it. He is so very fond of you, as you know. "Tell Mademoiselle Pauline," he said, "that the Tuileries is the very worst place for her to be. Both for her personal health and her political health as well."

Her political health? What did the man mean? I puzzled over that for a moment, then read on.

Papa has been elected mayor of the town and is very busy. But he says he is still concerned for you as your doctor, and will write at once to your mother to tell her you should leave Paris if you will but give him permission. Just say the word, my dear friend, and we'll have you back with us in the twinkling of an eye! As for me, I can't think what possible loyalty you can feel to people such as the ones you live among.

My eldest brother, Pierre – you remember him, Pauline, he is a lawyer – is now in Paris and sends us all the latest news. He writes that the freedoms gained by the people since July can never be taken away now. The King may struggle all he likes, but the new Assembly will soon take the last of his real power from him. If he objects too much, they may whisk the throne from under his fat behind!

"This . . . this is treason!" I cried, scowling at Pauline. Then I read on, while she buried her face in her hands.

As for the precious Queen you speak of so kindly, I must confess that I doubt your judgment. Pierre says it's criminal that the people go hungry while that wicked woman still spends thousands of livres a year on jewels and dresses.

What a cruel thing to say! It made Maman sound like some kind of monster. Why she hadn't bought any dresses or jewels for – well, months. I crumpled the letter into a ball and threw it in Pauline's face. "How *dare* you!" I said, my voice shaking. "You . . . you traitor! You sneak! You sit here all mealy-mouthed pretending to be our friend and yet you encourage people to write this way about us!"

"Please, Madame, please," begged Pauline. "Don't tell my mother!"

"*Your* mother! You'd better hope I don't tell *my* mother!"

Tears streamed down Pauline's face. "Please let me explain," she sobbed.

"I don't want to hear it!" I stormed out of the room, banging the door behind me.

Then I stopped. I *did* want to hear it. What possible excuse could Perfect Pauline give, after all?

So I stormed back and planted myself in front of her. "Make your excuses, then," I demanded. "And after that I'll tell you what I'm going to do about this! And, *parbleu*, please blow your nose."

Pauline obeyed. Her face was red and swollen from crying. She wrung her damp handkerchief between her fingers and sat with her eyes cast down.

"Well?" I growled, tapping my foot on the floor. "Who is this . . . this person who dares to talk of her betters this way?"

"Her name is Sophie Duvernier," Pauline began in a small voice. "She's . . . Sophie's father is a doctor in the town near our estate. I had a bad fever a few years ago, and when our usual doctor couldn't help me, my mother called in Doctor Duvernier. Maman says he saved my life." She gave a huge sniff, and blew her nose again.

"After that I had to stay in bed a long time," she went on. "Months and months. And I was so wretched. My sisters were all grown up and married and Maman often had to be away. There was no one my age to talk to. So when Doctor Duvernier suggested his daughter might come and keep me company sometimes, my mother agreed, though of course they were not a noble family."

"That's plain enough!" I said.

"But it didn't matter," Pauline protested. "We just talked about . . . about ordinary things. Books. And fashions. And later, when I was better, we'd go out for walks and rides."

She glanced up defiantly. "I like her very much. She was my friend when I didn't have any others. So even later when I was well and started going into society, we still used to see each other whenever I was in the country. And we write to each other."

"So I see!" I glared at her.

"It's just lately, just this year, that Sophie's letters have become so . . . so . . . " Pauline broke off, then started again. "She's changed. She talks of nothing but politics now. Taxes, and the bad harvest, and how the King and Queen and the Church and the aristocrats are like leeches that drain the blood of the people!"

She shook her head. "I suppose it's the influence of her family. Her brother Pierre is a lawyer, as she says – and she always looked up to Pierre because he was older. Also, Doctor Duvernier has been a leading citizen of the town for years. Sophie used to joke about how he was always talking about politics. But she isn't joking anymore."

I twisted a strand of my hair, trying to take it all in. Pauline stopped speaking and sat gazing up at me. "What?" I asked.

"I said, 'What are you going to do now?' Are you going to tell my mother?"

What *was* I going to do? I considered. It was rather delicious after all. Pauline the paragon, caught being less than perfect. How could I make the most of it? I could tell on her, and she would certainly get into trouble. Most likely she'd be sent away . . .

No! I thought. Why should she go free when the rest of us have to stay cooped up here? So then, I couldn't tell, could I? There had to be another way.

I turned my back on her and walked over to the window, thinking rapidly. I'd wanted to know what was happening, hadn't I? Well, here was a way. Not a very nice way, but . . .

I turned around. "No," I said. "I'm not going to tell your mother. Or my mother. Or anybody."

Pauline breathed a sigh of relief, and a tinge of colour crept into her cheeks. "Thank you, Your Highness," she breathed.

"Oh, no," I said. "Don't thank me. I'm not done with you yet. There's a price for my silence. You must show me all of Sophie's letters from now on. And you're not to tell her you're showing me them, either."

Pauline stared at me. "But that's . . . not honourable. My letters are private."

I grinned. I couldn't help it. "Not anymore," I said. "Or they can stay private, and I'll go straight to your mother – and mine!"

And so it began. It wasn't long, though, before I wondered what I'd let myself in for.

8

Secrets

January – June 1790

Early in the New Year, Pauline approached me with one hand in her pocket and drew me aside.

"Sophie?" I asked.

She nodded.

I tucked my hand inside her elbow. "Come, Pauline," I said loudly. "Let's walk up and down a little. We'll be warmer that way."

Maman glanced up at us approvingly, no doubt pleased that I was being nice to her pet for once. Little did she know!

When we reached the far end of the room, Pauline slipped the paper into my hand. What other outrageous nonsense would this Sophie have written? My eyes ran greedily down the page. *Books . . . clothes . . . her father . . . her mother . . .* ah, here it was.

> *It is perhaps as well that you remain in Paris for now,* I read, *for the peasants are still rising in revolt*

in many places. Your mother's estate has not been harmed yet, but brigands might come into the district from somewhere else – who can tell? For though I love you well, it's true you and your family belong to the aristocracy that has drained our country of its lifeblood for so long!"

"So," I said. "You're a cursed aristo too, Pauline." I must have sounded pleased, because she smiled just a little. Then the word "Paris" caught my eye again.

Our dear Pierre sends such exciting news from Paris. He works with Citizen Danton, one of the most important revolutionaries. Pierre admires Danton tremendously. He says that Danton's not fooled, like some of the people, into thinking the King should still be the head of government. Danton says the King is not to be trusted, and that the people are idiots not to press for more change.

My hand clenched, crumpling the letter. "How dare he!" I cried. Than afraid the others might over-hear, I lowered my voice. "More sneers. More lies about Papa! How can the King of France not be trusted by his subjects?" I demanded.

Pauline blushed to the roots of her hair. "I don't know, Your Highness," she faltered. "But – "

"Don't tell me you mean to make excuses for this precious Sophie of yours!"

"No! But – "

"If you say 'but' one more time I'll . . . I'll scream," I threatened.

Pauline bit her lip.

I stood glaring at her for a moment, then my curiosity got the better of me. I smoothed out the paper and read on:

People think that the King is too much influenced by the Queen. They suspect the King would like the Queen's brother to come to her rescue and crush France. They even say that the Comte d'Artois has wicked plans of his own, now that he's safe abroad . . .

"Wicked plans!" I sneered. "Oncle Charles? Why, Maman says he has never planned anything more than a day at the races! And what does Sophie mean about rescue?"

"I . . . I think she means the Emperor of Austria might try to invade France to set your family free," said Pauline.

"And make the revolutionaries let us go back to Versailles?"

She nodded.

"Really? Then I wish the Emperor would hurry up about it!" I said, thinking of Marron.

I screwed the paper into a ball and stuffed it back in Pauline's pocket.

🍃 🍃 🍃

Winter wore on. A few of Maman's friends who lived in Paris dared to begin visiting us, and one day Maman announced that she wanted to give a tea party to entertain them. Some of them were invited to bring their children so Charles would have someone to play with. No one but Maman would have thought of such a thing in the midst of a revolution.

"Pauline has been good enough to offer to organize the games and entertainments for the children," Maman said. "You can make yourself useful by helping her."

As soon as I could get away from Maman, I sought out my favourite window seat and sat down to sulk. It was cold beside the glass, and the heavy old draperies smelled musty. But at least I could pull them across and have a private place to myself.

Pauline again, I thought glumly. Now Maman was trusting her to be in charge, and I had to help her!

And so we played games up and down the dingy corridors of the palace. Afterwards we drank honeyed almond-water and ate little sticky pink sugar cakes Pauline had ordered.

I quite liked the cakes, and ate more than a few of them, until Maman, gliding by, gave me a rap on the wrist with her fan.

"Don't stuff yourself, Mousseline," she hissed. "You'll end up as stout as your papa!" Then, smiling radiantly about her, she swept on.

As soon as the guests had gone, I fled to my window seat and yanked the draperies closed. Pulling my knees up, I wrapped my skirts around my feet. The party had been just as boring as I thought it would be!

Pauline sat with my mother and Louise awhile, laughing and chatting about the visitors. I wondered how they could find so much to say about such an empty-headed lot of people.

After a few minutes, though, the curtains twitched

open and there was Pauline. "Did you enjoy the party, Your Highness?" she asked, sitting down beside me.

"I enjoyed the cakes," I muttered.

"Yes, I thought so," she replied.

I glanced at her sideways. Was there the ghost of a smile on her face?

With a quick glance over her shoulder, Pauline pulled out a letter.

"Not another!" I protested. "This Sophie of yours must have ink running in her veins."

She shrugged. "Sophie's trying to educate me. She says it's good for me to know the truth of things."

Her version of it. Reluctantly I held out my hand. As before, I only scanned the letter. Sophie went on and on about the Revolution, as if it were the only thing that mattered in the whole world:

I wish you could share our joy, Pauline. Why, in less than a year our world has been turned upside down –

"Upside down! I exclaimed. "Now that's the truest word she has ever written. But can she really expect you to rejoice over that?"

Pauline shrugged. "Sophie is very . . . enthusiastic," she said. "She was always getting excited about things."

"She's quite mad," I muttered. But I went back to the letter all the same:

Papa says the cursed aristos and their party are plotting to overthrow the new government and put things back the way they were before. But it will never work. The foolish King and his she-wolf of a Queen are safely shut up where they can do no

harm. We shall have a democracy, like the United
States of America. We are creating a new and better
world, where there will be justice for all. At least,
that is what my papa and my brothers think, and
they must know . . .

I sighed and handed the letter back to Pauline.
"Can she really believe all this?" I asked. "That 'aristos' like you and your family are all wicked– and that
my father is a fool and my mother a she-wolf?"

Pauline nodded miserably. "She must. Sophie is
nothing if not frank."

After a moment I said, "And you, Pauline, what do
you think?"

She blushed, but her chin came up and she gazed
at me steadily. "I . . . I worry that the people seem to
suffer," she said. "But I know that my family, at least,
has never harmed anyone. As for Their Majesties, no
one who knows them as I do could think such things
about them."

I wondered about that. How many of even our
so-called friends really cared whether Papa went on
being King or not? Everyone knew that many people
at court had preferred my uncles to Papa, because
they were easier to talk to, it was said. Papa was
famous for his silences. It was easy for people to think
bad things about him. Sophie might be right, at least
about that.

"What is she like, this Sophie of yours?" I asked.

"Like?" Pauline looked at me, surprised.

"Is she tall, or short, or fat or – oh, I don't know.

Just tell me something about her."

Pauline considered. "Well, she's taller than you – "

"That's nothing. Everyone is. I suppose she's pretty, too?"

"She's more . . . interesting to look at. She has a pointed face, with a big nose, and green eyes. Lots of curly dark brown hair."

I considered. "But what does she like? Books and embroidery like you, I suppose?"

Pauline laughed. "Definitely *not* embroidery. She does love to read, but most of all she loves riding horses."

"Why, so do I," I said, surprised. "Anyway, you like her," I added flatly.

"Yes," said Pauline. "And, do you know something, Your Highness? I think you would, too, if you knew her."

"Never! How could I, when she calls my parents names like that?"

"Well, perhaps you could talk her out of it. She does say exactly what she thinks, though. Like you."

Like me? I was indignant. How dared Pauline compare me to this revolutionary ranter!

And yet . . . and yet . . . from that moment on I felt as if a big-nosed girl with curly hair and sharp green eyes was looking over my shoulder and into my thoughts.

🌿 🌿 🌿

At last, just when it seemed that winter would stay forever, spring came. Real spring, with the chestnut trees in the gardens holding up their white candles of bloom along the Seine. In April we received wonderful news. The Assembly would allow us to spend the summer at St. Cloud, a small palace in the countryside just beyond the gates of Paris.

Maman's mood, always like quicksilver, turned from gloom to delight in a moment. "How wonderful to be away from the noise and dirt of the city," she exclaimed. "We'll be able to walk and drive wherever we want without crowds gathering. Oh, it's too lovely!"

So we went. We took with us only the most necessary things, and the fewest possible people. With Charles gambolling ahead, and Pauline tagging after us, I explored every corner of St. Cloud. I gazed wide-eyed at the elegance of its blue, white and gold furnishings. They seemed so rich, so grand. Had I really always taken such luxury for granted?

Life at St. Cloud was so different from anything I'd known before. Because there weren't many of us, we all dined together with just a few servants around. And in the evenings we played billiards, which I was very bad at. Papa undertook to teach Pauline, who had never played before. She turned out to be as good at that as she was at everything else. Papa was delighted with her, and she was so proud to be playing against him. She vowed she'd tell her children and grandchildren about it someday. All this should have been another Sorrow to me, but somehow it wasn't.

Most days Papa had to go to Paris, where the Assembly was at work on the new Constitution. Sometimes the rest of us would go picnicking in the woods. More often, though, Maman would drive out in a carriage to visit friends in the countryside nearby, taking the Duchess and Charles with her. Pauline often went with them. As for me, I did my best to be left out of such boring trips. It meant I could do what I wanted, at least some of the time. I didn't have Marron, but sometimes I'd be taken out riding, or at least be allowed to visit the horses and feed them apples and sugar.

One hot afternoon, though, Pauline stayed behind with a headache. No one could take me riding, so after visiting the stables I had nothing more to do. I decided to rout Pauline out of her room.

"Oh, come along!" I said. "It will be much cooler down by the river, you know, and they'll never let me go on my own."

Not far from the riverbank, we came upon a grove of aspen trees, where two lion-faced fountains gushed water into a shallow stone basin. The laundresses of St. Cloud were at work, soaking and scrubbing the linens and hanging the sheets to dry on lines strung among the trees, where they flapped like white wings in the breeze.

"You see how cool it is?" I said, throwing myself down on the grass. Princesses aren't supposed to do that, but there was no one to stop me.

Pauline spread out her tiny lace-trimmed handkerchief and tried to sit down on it.

"Oh, bother your dress, Pauline," I groaned. "Who cares about grass stains?"

Pauline flushed. "Well, you know Maman . . . " But she pulled out the handkerchief and dropped it in her lap.

"You always do what your mother tells you, don't you?" I asked idly. I began picking daisies and weaving them into a chain.

"I suppose I do." Pauline bit her lip. "I'm the youngest in my family, so I'm used to people telling me what to do." She paused, then added, "I'm sure you must think I'm prim."

"Yes," I blurted out before I had a chance to think. "I mean . . . no. Not anymore, anyway."

Oddly enough, once I'd said the words, I realized they were true. "The way you're so perfect all the time does bother me," I admitted. "I used to think you were showing off, but now I think you can't help it. You're just naturally good. And . . . and I wish I could be more like you."

Pauline stared. "You think that about me? Why, Madame, I thought you hated me!"

Now I'd started, I rushed to explain. "Oh, no, Pauline, I never hated you," I said. "Though I used to think you were one of my Sorrows. I just wish I were as clever as you are, that's all. There isn't anything you can't do – you're even good at billiards. And I can't help feeling jealous sometimes because Maman and Charles have got so very fond of you."

"Jealous of *me*? But you're a princess!"

"Not much fun in that," I said gloomily. "Too much etiquette." I didn't mention my other Sorrows.

Half-embarrassed, we were silent for a moment. Then Pauline reached into her pocket and pulled out a letter.

I felt almost hurt. Would I never live that down? How she must hate me for making her show them to me! Why had I ever made her do it in the first place? It was so mean!

"Oh, put it away, Pauline!" I said. "You don't have to show me any more of them. I won't tell on you."

"I know you won't," she replied, still holding out the letter. "I've known that for a long time now. But I *want* you to see them."

I gaped at her. "You do?"

"Yes. At first I didn't. But I felt so guilty before, you see. Getting letters like that . . . in secret. I begged Sophie not to write me such things, but . . . " She shrugged. "Well, by now you know Sophie. Of course, she doesn't know you read the letters too."

"Just as well," I said. "I imagine she'd have some choice things to say about princesses as well as kings and queens."

I'd come to look on the letters as a dose of medicine I had chosen to take, but that didn't mean I had to like it. Reading them always made me feel as if Sophie was peering over my shoulder again. Still, I felt a sneaking interest in what outrageous thing she would say next. I unfolded the paper and began to read:

We are all very busy planning the celebrations for the new Constitution in July. Maman and I have new dresses, in the very latest fashion – simple and

straight, with no bushy petticoats underneath. Oh, I
know you will smile, and think I only care about
having a new dress, Pauline. But it's more than that.
The new styles are just one more way to show how
the world has changed from the old days. The men's
fashions are new too, you know. They all wear loose
trousers now – no more knee breeches like the ones
the aristos wear.

"So they're even revolutionizing clothing," I
mused. "What next?"

The letter went on:

Of course there will be a much greater fête for
the Constitution in Paris. Pierre writes that the King
will attend, but after all, what he does no longer
matters. All the real power in the land is in the
hands of the Assembly . . .

My heart sank. Was it really true? Didn't Papa even
matter anymore? What use was it to be king if you
didn't matter? And why – why? – did I have to be told
by someone who hated us?

I handed the letter back to Pauline, and sat with
my eyes cast down, plucking at the grass.

"It has made you sad," she said, tucking the letter
away. "I'm sorry."

"Well, I asked for it, didn't I?" I said, miserably. "It's
all such a muddle. I just wish everything could be as
it was before."

"I know," Pauline said.

It sounded as if she really cared. My eyes suddenly
filled with tears, and I gave a huge sniff. What would

my old macaw say if she could see me snivelling? Princesses weren't supposed to show their feelings. Well, I couldn't help it. Too bad for etiquette.

Pauline held out her handkerchief.

I wiped my eyes and blew my nose, feeling foolish. I started binding my daisy chain into a wreath. After working at it for a few minutes I said, "See here, Pauline, I'm . . . I'm glad you came to live with us. I mean, I'm sorry you had to leave your home. You must have hated that. And then all these terrible things happened. How you must have wished your mother had never agreed to become our governess! But for us, for me, I'm glad."

"I did hate it at first," Pauline admitted. "Or, at least, I was so nervous and afraid I'd do something wrong that I thought I hated it."

"You certainly never looked nervous," I said, glancing at her. "But then, I suppose you're just naturally calm and composed, like your mother."

Pauline laughed. "Oh, I'm not like Maman. Not a bit! She really is calm and steady all the way through. Just like a rock. Now me, I sometimes quiver inside like a jelly. It's all I can do to keep my outside looking steady."

"I wish I could do even that," I said ruefully. "I can't seem to help showing how I feel. One way or the other."

"It doesn't matter. You're honest. And you're very brave," said Pauline. "I know. I saw you that horrible time at Versailles. I was watching from a window when you went out on the balcony, you know."

"Well, I didn't have any choice about that," I said with a sigh. "Going out there was the last thing I wanted to do. Anyway, I don't *feel* brave. And I wish I didn't have to be. If we can't go back to Versailles, I wish we could all stay here at St. Cloud forever."

"Yes," Pauline agreed, with a huge smile. "And play billiards!"

I laughed. I couldn't help it. She was prouder of that than of all her proper accomplishments. On impulse, I reached over and set my daisy wreath on her hair. Then I scrambled to my feet and held out my hand to her.

We wandered back through the sunny gardens. As we reached the terrace, I held her back a moment. "We can be friends, now, can't we?" I asked. "Real friends?"

"Of course we can," said Pauline.

"Maman has always had so many friends," I added as we went on. "But I've never had one at all. Until now."

"Shall I be just like Louise de Lamballe?" teased Pauline.

I pretended to think it over. "No," I said at last. "You don't have to faint *quite* so often!"

We burst into giggles, and even the stiff National Guardsman at the door grinned at us through his fierce moustache.

9

Caged

July – November 1790

It was hard, so hard, to go back to Paris after our glorious golden weeks at St. Cloud. But we had to, for delegates were coming from all over France to celebrate the new Constitution. It seemed to me, though, that what they really wanted was to have a good look at Papa and the rest of us. By the hundreds and thousands they poured through the Tuileries, day after day, to gaze at us.

"Long live our good Papa King!" they cried, "And our Dauphin!"

Charles, all blue eyes and blond curls, very quickly learned how to make pretty little speeches to them. Everyone found him enchanting. He was very good at it, though he was still only five.

As for me, I hated every moment of it, but I smiled and smiled. Four-tooth smiles, too.

There was a great ceremony to celebrate the signing of the Constitution. Maman had herself and Tante Babet and me all done up in white muslin dresses in the latest style, with tricolour sashes and bows. As if fashion would change people's minds about us.

The morning of the *fête* dawned dark and dripping with rain, but just as the ceremony began the sun broke through, gleaming on the white robes of the priest and the brilliant colours of the flags and the sashes of the National Guards.

A murmur sped through the crowd below the balcony we stood on. "It's an omen, a good omen!" People nudged each other and began to smile. Then the vast crowd raised their hands and swore loyalty to the French nation, its new constitution, and its king.

I felt tears spring to my eyes. Let it truly be a new beginning, I wished fiercely. Let the Revolution be over at last!

But it was not to be. By autumn there were rumours of war. Sophie's letters said people everywhere were accusing Papa and Maman of conspiring to betray France and destroy the new republican army. I was bewildered. The people had seemed to love us in the summer. Why were they saying such horrible things now?

The newspaper headlines, cried under our windows by the vendors, said that Maman was pleading with the Emperor of Austria to invade France and slaughter the revolutionaries.

The Duchess caught me listening one day, and told me not to be so foolish.

"But they're saying such awful things," I said.

She looked disdainful. "These Parisians are a fickle lot. They run mad at every outrageous rumour. By tomorrow they will have forgotten it all."

Remembering Sophie's letters, I wasn't so sure. She made it very clear that it wasn't just the Parisians who were against us. She talked about how revolutionaries were meeting in every town in France.

To make things worse, it was as if anger and confusion had crept into our own hearts. Papa, my kind Papa, was grumpy with all of us, and his silences sometimes went on for hours. As for Maman, she scolded him for his gloominess and lack of energy, and often made brittle jokes at his expense. How I hated that! He was like a poor bear in a cage – it was cruel to tease him.

More than once I found her speaking fiercely to him in a low voice, holding a letter in her hand. I wondered about those letters. These days she seemed to do little else but write letters and receive them.

I was in her room one day, summoned for some small fault she wanted to correct me about. I found her sitting at her desk, which was piled high with papers. Someone opened a door and the infamous draughts of the Tuileries did the rest. A cloud of papers rose from her desk and fluttered down onto the carpet.

I stooped to pick them up, but Maman hurried to seize them herself. "Leave them!" she said sharply. I handed back the few I'd picked up, glancing at the top sheet as I did so. What I saw riveted my eyes to the page. The letter was in some sort of code!

"Give it to me!" Maman demanded, holding out her hand. Her eyes bored into mine, as if seeking to discover my thoughts. Then, "Go away, child," she added, less sharply. "I'm too busy to deal with you now."

I fled to my window seat, my thoughts in a whirl. Were the newspapers right? Was she really trying to get the Emperor to make war on France by sending him military secrets? Was she that afraid? I feared that she might be. For it was clear how much she felt the strain of our long months of captivity. She had become thin and nervous, and her once-glossy golden hair was dull and threaded with grey at the temples.

But if foreign countries defeated France, it would break Papa's heart. I couldn't believe he would ever connive at such a thing. Never! But did he know all that Maman was doing?

There was no answer to that, or to any of my other questions.

My father and my aunt quarrelled too. On my way to visit Tante Babet in her rooms one morning, I blundered into the midst of one of their arguments.

"I won't have it, Babet!" Papa roared. "If our brother Charles doesn't understand that this wild talk of getting foreign powers to invade the country is ridiculous, he could ruin everything for us – and for France!"

"But Louis, you must do something!" Tante Babet's

voice was sharp. "We can't just wait for them to cut our throats! They have caged us! And every day the more extreme revolutionaries are making wilder and wilder demands."

"I will never, *never* agree to an invasion that will spill the blood of my people! Keep that in mind, Madame," growled my father.

"Let us hope your people will be equally scrupulous about *your* blood," Tante Babet shot back.

Then they caught sight of me, standing frozen in the doorway.

"What are you hanging about for, Thérèse?" Papa thundered.

Papa had never used that tone of voice to me. Startled, I took a step backward.

"Oh, leave the child alone, Louis," said Tante Babet wearily. "She only came to visit me, after all. You never do that anymore, except to quarrel!"

Papa shrugged impatiently. With a scowl on his face, he tramped away down the corridor.

Tante Babet flounced into a chair near the window. She was still angry. I could tell by the high colour in her cheeks, and the way she twitched at the lace of her *fichu*.

I went over and sat down on a low stool beside her. "Tante Babet, what's wrong?" I asked, placing my hand on her knee. "You and Papa never used to fight before."

She sighed, and patted my hand. "Oh, child, you can't possibly understand," she said.

Suddenly anger and frustration boiled up inside me. I jerked my hand away. "I'm *not* a child," I said, glaring at her. "*Charles* is a child – he never worries about anything. But I do!"

She looked at me, startled. "Perhaps you're right," she said. "All of us forget how fast you're growing up. But what can you possibly make of it all?"

"More than you guess," I said eagerly. "I – " Then I had to bite my tongue. I'd nearly blurted out the secret of Sophie's letters! "I . . . I listen to the news criers," I said instead. "Even though the Duchess tells me not to. And sometimes I see newspapers . . . "

My aunt cocked her head, a habit of hers when she was curious about something. "Does it matter so much to you, then?" she asked.

"Yes!" I cried. "Don't you think it should?"

Tante Babet nodded slowly. "Yes, of course it should. It's your life that's being ruined too, after all. We grown-ups are so caught up in our own sorrows that it's easy for us to forget that."

"So why are you and Papa fighting, then?" I mumbled, half-embarrassed, but still determined to find out.

"Well. How can I explain it to you?" Tante Babet thought for a moment. "Your papa has agreed to new laws – taxes, restricted powers, that sort of thing. It's complicated, Mousseline, but what it amounts to is that the measures harm the holy Church. I can never, never agree to accept such laws." She paused. "Oh, Louis didn't want to agree to them either, but he gave in to the revolutionaries' demands. He seems to think that giving in will appease them. I think otherwise!"

She paused, then went on. "There's more. Your papa thinks I favour your uncle Charles too much." She smiled. "You must understand, Mousseline, that this has always been so. You know how handsome and full of life your uncle is. I've worshipped him since I was a child. And Louis has always minded."

It was true. Oncle Charles was everything Papa was not – handsome, and witty and lively. Slim, too. I had a flash of understanding. Papa must be jealous of his brother! I surely knew how that felt.

"Your uncle Charles is eager to act against the Revolution," Tante Babet said. "He is trying to bring foreign armies to our aid. And he encourages loyal people in France to rise up against this illegal govenment that has imprisoned us. He wants to make things the way they used to be before all this began. And so do I!" she finished, her eyes flashing.

That didn't seem so wrong. I wanted things back the way they were before too – if only the people could have enough to eat, and not hate us anymore. But . . . "What does papa say?" I asked.

My aunt shrugged. "Your father doesn't say what he plans to do. Perhaps he doesn't even know himself," she said bitterly. "He has tried to work with this abominable Revolution. He has signed the new Constitution that takes most of his power away, and now he insists he must stand by it. Yet he sees daily that the revolutionaries aren't satisfied. The more he grants, the more they demand." Her voice was growing sharp again. "Where will it all end? No wonder he's been growling at us all lately!"

I didn't know what to say. Papa was the King, and no one except Maman ever criticized him. Still, Tante Babet was his little sister. Maybe she knew him better than any of the rest of us did, after all.

As usual, my face gave away my feelings.

"Now I've shocked you, Mousseline," said my aunt, getting up. She kissed me on the forehead. "Enough of all this. Go now, and leave me to my prayers. That is one duty I can still perform for our poor country."

By the time I reached the door, she was already on her knees before her little *prie-dieu*, her head bowed over her rosary.

Needless to say, I made more of a mess of my lessons than usual that afternoon. Afterward I sat in my window seat, brooding. Though it was really *our* window seat now, the place where Pauline and I curled up behind the curtains to share letters or just escape the eyes of the grown-ups for awhile.

Pauline soon slipped through the curtains to join me.

"What's wrong?" she asked gently.

"Sorrows," I told her.

Sorrows, indeed. How petty my old list looked now, compared to this heartache. I felt as if the world was turned upside down – just as Sophie had once said. Papa was the King. He had always been like the sun, with all of us planets circling around him. Despite

Tante Babet's stinging words, I still couldn't doubt him. Not really. Surely, surely he must know best what to do for France. Tante Babet and Oncle Charles and Maman must be wrong. Mustn't they?

But what if they weren't?

"You know, Pauline, if it weren't for you I think I would run mad," I said. "All my family are cross with each other. I feel as if I'm being pulled apart, and I'm of no earthly use to anyone."

"You're of use to *me*," said my dear gazelle.

10

Turned Back

December 1790 – March 1791

Christmas was a sad, dark time. Almost all our old friends had fled away abroad again, except for the faithful Louise. Yet somehow the winter wore on, and at last some days of pale sunshine told us that spring wasn't far away.

Not long before Easter, Pauline and I were doing lessons when Madame de Tourzel appeared in the doorway. "Your pardon, Madame," she said to me. Then, "Pauline, please come to my room for a moment. I must speak with you."

With a puzzled glance at me, Pauline got up. A quarter of an hour later, she returned, her eyes suspiciously red. Without a word, she bent her head over her German grammar, but I could see that she was only pretending to study it.

I reached over and flipped the book shut. "Now don't *you* start hiding things, Pauline. What is it?

What's the matter?"

"I'm being sent away!"

"But why? What has happened?"

"My mother insists that my health is in danger from the cold and damp here. I'm to go to stay with my married sisters in the country and not come back until Maman sends for me again."

I was dumbfounded. "Go away! You mustn't. I can't do without you!" But the moment I said the words I could have bitten my tongue.

Pauline's pale cheeks flushed and she burst into tears. "You must think I'm like all those others who have deserted you," she sobbed. "I begged Maman to let me stay, but she won't even talk about it. She said it was all arranged."

We gazed miserably at each other. Then I said gruffly, "Your mother is right, you know. It's still terribly damp and cold here. And you've had a bad cough all winter. You must go away where it's warmer and get well. And . . . and before you know it, it'll be summer again, and we'll all be together at St. Cloud."

"Dear St. Cloud. We had such good times there!"

"And we will again," I promised, squeezing her hand. "Billiards every single night." I'd hoped to make her smile, but I only made it worse.

She began to weep again. "Oh, Madame, I'll be so worried about you! Well, all of you, but you especially."

I swallowed an enormous lump in my throat and croaked, "Oh, I'll be all right. And you can write and tell me everything you see and do." Trying to make a joke, I added, "I love letters – surely you know that by now!"

"I'll write you every single day!" Pauline vowed.

Two days later, she was gone.

❦ ❦ ❦

"My sisters overwhelm me with kindness, and I am growing quite fat on country cream," I read aloud. *"But I would far rather be with you in Paris."*

"I wish she were here, too," Charles complained. "Pauline's much better at trictrac than you are, Mousseline." He leaned against my arm and peered at the letter. "Does she say she misses *me* very much?"

"Well, not exactly," I said.

"Mon dieu, how strange! Because I know she loves me best."

"Oh she does, does she? You vain little cockerel!" I pounced on him and tickled him.

He wriggled away and ran off, calling over his shoulder, "Don't be jealous, Mousseline. Pauline loves you *next* best."

I was counting the days until Easter, for after that I could hope we would leave for St. Cloud. And after that would come summer, and then surely Pauline would come back. Beyond summer, I wouldn't think.

At last it was Easter Sunday. We were to leave for St. Cloud the next day. By Monday noon we were itching to be away.

"Goodbye, gloomy Tuileries! Goodbye, goodbye, goodbye! We won't see you for months!" Charles and

95

I seized each others' hands and galloped madly up and down the room. Madame de Tourzel came in to see what the noise was about, and gave me The Look. But then she relented, and smiled at our giddiness.

"Excuse us, Duchess," I panted, feeling rather silly. "It's just that we're half crazy with joy. We've looked forward to this for so long."

Down the broad main staircase we went. Charles was still prancing, but I tried to walk sedately, though I couldn't help giving a little skip now and then. Papa and Maman and Tante Babet were waiting, all smiles for once. I ran to hug each of them. I just knew that by leaving Paris we would put our sorrows behind us.

The great double doors swung open, and a vast uneasy murmuring enveloped us, a sound like the wind, like the sea. And there was the white rat general, wearing as many medals and ribbons as ever. He swung down from his tall white stallion and met us at the foot of the stairs.

"What is it, General? Is there trouble?" Papa asked.

The general looked puzzled. "I scarcely know, Your Majesty. All has been quiet. The carriages await you. But suddenly this crowd has assembled outside the gates. I suspect it's some plot to stir up people's suspicions. At any rate, the people swear they will not let you pass."

"Impossible!" said Papa. "The Assembly has ruled that we may go. I trust you'll do your duty?"

"Indeed, Your Majesty," said the general, saluting. "Please take your seats in the carriages. If you seem determined, it should carry the day."

The gates swung open ahead of us, and the crowd swirled into the courtyard. General Lafayette ordered his troops to clear a way through for us, but hands seized the bridles of the horses, causing them to plunge and rear in panic.

"The King cannot leave!" rough voices shouted. "We won't let him!"

Papa put his head out the carriage window, and said loudly, "I have given the nation its liberty. May I not be free myself?"

"You'll not run away from us!" someone cried. "You go to hatch treacherous plots at St. Cloud!"

"Oui!" a ragged chorus agreed.

Other voices howled, "Fat pig! Miserable aristo! You will do as we say!"

Angry at these insults, my father's gentlemen-in-waiting placed themselves around the carriage to protect us. The crowd fell upon them, kicking and beating them savagely.

One young courtier, a favourite with Charles, fell to the ground covered with blood. "Save him, save my *pauvre* Rocheforte!" Charles screamed. Maman seized Charles tightly in her arms and covered his eyes with her hand.

I cowered on my seat as abuse and insults swirled around us. Then a flicker of anger leapt up inside me, driving back fear. How *dared* they insult Papa so? I sat up straight and glared out the window at the furious faces around us.

General Lafayette ordered his troops to push the crowd back, but many of his National Guardsmen stood aside, refusing to obey. Then, forcing his mount through the crowd, he leaned close to the carriage window and shouted to Papa above the din. "I have enough loyal troops to break through, if Your Majesty will permit me to fire on the crowd," he said.

To give him his due, he actually looked as if he meant it.

There was a long pause. Then Papa bowed his head. "I cannot do that," he said at last. "If we must stay to avoid bloodshed, then we must."

My mother's eyes flashed, and she bit her lip.

Papa is wrong, wrong! I thought in anguish. Can't he see they will only think he is weak? But then, if he did order his people shot wouldn't he truly be the tyrant the revolutionaries said he was? Was there no answer at all?

I was sick with anger, shame and pity for Papa's helplessness.

There was nothing for it but to make our way back to the palace, through lines of National Guardsmen who held the jeering crowd back. Papa went first. Tante Babet, her face stony, stalked behind him, holding my hand. Maman followed, carrying the sobbing Charles.

As we crossed the threshold, my mother shot a furious glance at Papa. "Now at last even you must admit we're no longer free," she said coldly. "So much for your precious Constitution!"

Papa said nothing. With drooping shoulders and bent head he trudged ahead of us up the long, steep stairs.

11

Flight

The June night was stiflingly hot, but even without the heat I wouldn't have been able to sleep. That afternoon Maman had taken me aside and whispered that we were going to have an adventure.

"An adventure! But what? When?" I asked.

Maman shook her head. "No questions. All will be explained later. Just behave as usual, and say nothing to anyone. Remember, we are surrounded by spies!"

So of course I couldn't sleep. I tossed and turned, but was still wide awake when, not long after ten o'clock, Maman came into my room carrying a lighted candle. I sat up and stared at her in amazement, for I had never seen her looking like this before.

She was dressed in a plain grey gown underneath a black mantle, and her hair was covered by a large hat with a veil. If I hadn't known who she was, I'd have taken her for a servant. Behind her was one of her maids, her arms full of clothing.

"Hurry, Mousseline," Maman whispered. "It's time for our adventure. Put on these clothes Émilie has brought."

The gown Émilie handed me was of green muslin with little blue flowers on it. Quite pretty, really, but nothing like the silk ones I was used to. Émilie and I followed my mother to Madame de Tourzel's rooms, where the Duchess and Charles were waiting.

To my astonishment, Charles was dressed as a girl!

He was furious. "They said we'd be going where there were soldiers," he muttered. "I asked for my sword and uniform, but they gave me this."

"You look very pretty, Charles," I teased. He scowled, so I added quickly, "After all, it's only dressing up, like putting on a play."

"Now children, listen very carefully," said Maman. "Mousseline is right, this is just like a play and we must all act our parts. We're going on a journey, and Madame de Tourzel will play the part of Madame de Korff, a Russian lady. You must pretend to be her children and call her 'Maman.' Can you remember that, both of you?"

We nodded.

"I'm playing the part of your governess," Maman went on. "Papa will be Madame de Korff's valet, and your Tante Babet will be a maid. If we're stopped for any reason, and you're questioned, you must swear that this is true. Do you understand?"

"Yes, Maman," we both said solemnly. It was something new to be told we must tell lies!

Madame de Tourzel looked at her pocket watch. "It's time, Your Majesty," she said.

"You must not call me that, Madame. Not now," my mother cautioned her.

We stole down a back staircase to a courtyard where a shabby-looking carriage stood waiting. The driver sat slouched behind the reins like any common fellow, but as we came up he raised the brim of his hat slightly, and I recognized the clear blue eyes and handsome face of Comte Axel de Fersen. He sprang down and held open the door as Charles and I and Madame de Tourzel clambered in.

The door clicked shut behind us. "Maman, aren't you coming too?" I said, leaning out the open window.

My mother put her finger to her lips. "Shhh, Mousseline! Keep your voice down. Not yet. It's too dangerous if we all leave at once. Tante Babet will come to meet you soon, and your father and I after that." Then, wrapping her mantle more closely about her, she flitted back across the courtyard and disappeared into the palace.

With a jolt, the carriage rolled off across the cobblestones and out into the dark streets of Paris. We turned so many corners that I became quite muddled about the direction. At last we drew up on one side of a square and waited. After some minutes, we heard the clatter of horses' hooves and the jingle of harness in the distance.

Madame de Tourzel looked worried. "It sounds like soldiers," she murmured.

"Soldiers!" Charles was thrilled. He bounced up and tried to see, but the Duchess pushed him down onto the floor of the cab. "You must hide under my skirts, Your Highness," she whispered. "If we are noticed and you are recognized, all will be lost."

"But – "

The Look silenced Charles. Grumbling, he obeyed.

I pulled the hood of my mantle close about my face and peered out. The sounds grew louder, and torches flared in the darkness. Were they searching for us already?

"It's General Lafayette," said Madame de Tourzel in a low voice. "He must be enroute to attend His Majesty. I don't think they're looking for us."

I suddenly realized I had been holding my breath, and let it out in a long sigh of relief. Of course! General Lafayette, like all the officials of the royal court, always attended Papa's *coucher*, a kind of formal going-to-bed ceremony. Papa couldn't possibly slip away until that was over.

The soldiers passed along the far side of the square and disappeared into a side street. Again the carriage was wrapped in darkness. Minutes passed, then we heard the sound of footsteps coming nearer and nearer. Madame de Tourzel and I shrank back into the depths of the carriage. Then the footsteps stopped, and someone took hold of the handle of the carriage door.

There was a moment of awful silence as it swung open, then Madame de Tourzel said softly, "Thank God! It's you, Madame."

"Your maid, reporting for duty, Madame de Korff," said Tante Babet's voice. I squeezed over to make room for her. There was an indignant squeak as she trod on Charles, who was still hiding under Madame de Tourzel's skirts. Smothering nervous laughter, we pulled him out.

Scarcely had Tante Babet got settled than my father arrived, out of breath from his swift walk through the streets.

"Nothing to it," he said, pleased. "General Lafayette saw me retire. The moment he left I nipped into my valet's room and dressed in my disguise. Then out I went, right through the main door, and here I am. Antoinette should be here any minute too."

But Maman didn't come. A church clock chimed the quarter hour, then the half.

"What on earth can have gone wrong?" murmured Tante Babet. "She should have been here long ago."

I felt a dreadful leaden knot growing in the pit of my stomach. If they caught Maman outside the palace they might kill her!

Another quarter struck, and then the hour. It was midnight. Silence closed around us again. Then came the sound of hurrying feet. In a moment one of Papa's guards swung the door open and helped Maman mount the step.

She sank trembling onto the seat. Turning back her veil, she covered her face with her hands. "We got lost," she said. "It was a nightmare. The streets are so dark and twisting. We took a wrong turning and couldn't find our way. It felt as if we were wandering for hours!"

"It was quite long enough," muttered Papa, rapping on the roof of the cab to signal Comte Fersen to drive on.

As we moved off, Maman began to laugh in a strange, shaky way. "I even saw Lafayette himself," she gasped. "His carriage passed so close beside me in the street that I could have touched it. I was terrified, but at the same time I wanted to laugh. What a surprise is in store for him tomorrow!"

"You mean today," said my father. "It's past midnight. Pray that nothing more goes wrong."

Squeezed tightly into a corner, I peered out at the dark narrow streets of Paris. Only the lanterns of a few solitary passersby made little islands of light in the gloom. It looked sinister, and the rattle of our wheels on the cobblestones seemed loud enough to wake the whole city. I was afraid some mob would storm out of a side street to challenge us.

But our carriage passed unnoticed through the St. Martin gate on the east side of the city. Once outside, though, there were more anxious moments while Comte Fersen tried to find the larger carriage that would carry us for the rest of our journey. At last he found it, drawn up in an out-of-the-way spot under cover of some trees, and the cab pulled alongside. We climbed over into the new carriage without ever setting foot on the ground. By that time I was so worn out that I fell fast asleep as we rolled smoothly eastward into the dark countryside.

I awoke, hours later, to the pale light of morning. I rubbed my eyes, and stared at my parents.

"Well, my Mousseline. What do you think of our adventure?" my father asked, pinching my cheek.

"I was frightened to death until you all came," I confessed. "But where are we going now?"

"To Montmédy, my dear. I'll gather my loyal troops about me and then perhaps the Assembly will realize it must respect the rights it has granted me under the Constitution." Turning to Maman, he added, "Just let me get astride my horse and I'll be a very different fellow than the one you've seen lately!"

"It will inspire us all, I'm sure, Louis," Maman said gaily. "But for now, perhaps you and the children are ready for a bite of breakfast? I'm sure Comte Fersen has thought of everything."

And so he had. There was a basket packed with cold chicken, and bread, and meat pies. There were grapes and early strawberries, and bottles of wine and almond water to drink. We set to hungrily, laughing and talking as the sun came up over the fields, and the larks began to sing in the meadows around us.

What a holiday it was, after our long months in the Tuileries. Later, we even stopped for a few minutes so Charles could stretch his legs and pick wildflowers for Maman.

"It won't matter that we're a little late arriving at our rendezvous with the troops, my dears," Papa said. "I've sent a courier on ahead to let them know we're on our way. We should meet them at Châlons, or if not there, at Sainte Ménéhoulde."

But no troops waited for us at either place. We went on to Clermont, where we stopped to change horses. As they were being harnessed, a man sidled up to the carriage. "For God's sake drive on quickly," he whispered to my father. "Your plan is discovered!"

"Drive on at once!" ordered Papa, and the carriage lumbered forward on the road to Varennes.

I must have fallen asleep, for I was awakened by rough voices crying, "Stop! Stop!" There was a glare of light around the carriage. Hands seized the horses' bridles, and we rocked to a halt. Peering out, I saw a crowd of men with lighted torches. One man was holding his torch right up in Papa's face as he leaned out.

"Is it him? Is it the King?" cried a dozen voices.

"Good people," said Papa, "I am only the valet of Madame de Korff. Here are our passports. They are perfectly in order. Pray let us go on our way."

"Let's have a good look at them," someone shouted. "Get them all out!" The men levelled their guns at the carriage. Reluctantly Papa stepped down, and the rest of us followed.

"To the mayor's house!"

A large crowd gathered, buzzing with curiosity. Men bearing torches opened a way through for us. The bell of the local church began to clang, calling still more people into the streets. Remembering my part in our charade, I stayed close to Madame de

Tourzel, pretending she was my mother. I had to pinch Charles to remind him to do the same.

The mayor's house was brightly lit. The first thing I saw in the main chamber was a large portrait of Papa hanging on the wall. The people in the room eyed it too. They glanced back and forth trying to decide if the silk-clad figure in the painting was indeed the same as the man standing before them in a plain round hat and valet's clothes. No one was sure. Monsieur Sausse, the mayor, fumbled with our passports. He found nothing wrong with them, and said we could go.

But at that moment a man wearing the tricolour cockade rushed in. He stared Papa fiercely in the face for a moment, then swung round on the mayor and declared, "It's him! It's Louis himself! My name is Mangin, and I've seen him in Paris. If you let him escape, Monsieur le Maire, your life will be forfeit!"

Alarmed, Monsieur Sausse turned to Papa. "It couldn't . . . Are you really . . . ? Your Majesty?" he stammered.

Papa stood silent for a moment. Then his shoulders sagged. "I am your king," he admitted.

To my astonishment, most of the people in the room dropped at once to their knees, including poor Monsieur Sausse.

Mangin remained standing. "A fine king," he sneered, "running away from his people."

From all over the room, voices began to cry out in protest. "Yes! Why do you seek to leave us? A king should not flee from his people!"

I flinched. Was it wrong of Papa to try to run away? But they had treated him so badly in Paris!

"I never sought to leave my people," Papa replied. "I only sought to escape from the insults heaped upon me daily in Paris. Our destination is Montmédy, where I propose to live until the Assembly can guarantee my freedom."

"Don't believe him, good citizens," shouted Mangin. "He was fleeing across the frontier, where his wife's brother is waiting to give him an army. An army intending to murder French citizens!"

"*Never!*" Papa cried. "I would never leave France or harm my people!" But his voice was drowned by a chorus of cries and reproaches.

It was terribly hot in the midst of the crowd. I began to feel faint, and leaned on Tante Babet, who put her arm around me. Waves of sound from inside, from outdoors, beat against my ears. As though from far away I heard her cry, "Will no one take pity on the children? They're dropping with exhaustion. Can someone find them a bed?" And then I was being lifted and carried up some stairs, and laid down somewhere soft.

I slept fitfully, with voices breaking into my dreams. A man's voice, hard and determined. "Sire, you have a few loyal guards left near this town. Let me send them orders to fire on the crowd."

Then Papa's voice, low and sad. "No. It would be asking them to throw their lives away. The crowd is too large now. It would tear them to pieces." A pause, then, "We must wait. General de Bouillé cannot be far away with the troops that were supposed to meet us."

My mother's voice, high and strained. "Louis, you must do *something!*"

"What *can* I do, Antoinette?"

Too weary to listen more, I curled myself against Charles's warm little body and at last slept deeply.

I woke again with the first grey light of morning. Outside, the baying of the crowd had formed itself into a chant: "Long Live the Nation! The National Assembly! The King to Paris!"

Madame Sausse, a plump, kindly woman, insisted we have to eat something. So, travel-stained and weary, we all sat down to a large breakfast which none of us really wanted.

At last Papa threw down his napkin. "I can delay no longer," he said heavily. "Bouillé isn't coming. We must go back."

Back. It was worse than anything we had lived through before. From six in the morning until three in the afternoon we were not allowed to set foot out of the carriage. At every village jeering crowds surrounded us, reproaching Papa and insulting Maman. We sweltered in the closed carriage, but when we raised the blinds to let in a little air we let in more abuse, along with choking clouds of dust.

The next day we met Barnave and Pétion, two representatives of the Assembly who had ridden out from Paris. They squeezed themselves into our already-crowded carriage. Maman had to take Charles on her lap, while I half-sat, half-leaned against Tante Babet.

Pétion was rude and nasty, but Barnave seemed kinder. Wearily, I tried my old game: With his hooked nose, he looked like a bird of some kind. An eagle? No, more like an owl.

Charles took a deep interest in the motto on the brass buttons on Barnave's coat. "Live Free or Die," he recited, proud to show off his reading. "But what does it mean?"

"It means that anything is better than losing your freedom," Barnave replied seriously.

"Something you might bear in mind when you reproach my brother for trying to leave Paris," Tante Babet shot back.

"Yes!" agreed Maman, nodding at Barnave.

At last, on the third day, we reached the gates of Paris. A vast crowd was waiting, but this time they were silent, not shouting. Drums echoed a funeral beat, and the lines of soldiers on either side held their muskets upside down as a sign of dishonour. In the flaring torchlight we rolled through a forest of eyes. Not a single man raised his hat, not a single woman curtsied. The children simply gaped open-mouthed as we passed. The clink of harness, the sound of the horses' hooves echoed in the silence, and even the tall stone houses that leaned out over the street seemed to stare and condemn.

Charles stood up and looked out the carriage window for awhile. "Papa," he said, turning away, "why are the people so quiet? Why is the music so sad?"

My father said nothing.

"Papa's very tired, *chou d'amour*. You mustn't pester him now," said Maman wearily.

At the Tuileries, General Lafayette sat waiting for us astride his white stallion. As we stepped down he dismounted, sweeping off his plumed hat with a flourish. "Welcome back, Sire," he said. But his smile was cold, and his eyes were angry.

Filthy, exhausted, we made our way back to our rooms. I found hard-eyed strangers waiting to attend me. Every single person I'd known was gone.

"What day is it?" I asked dazedly, as they peeled off my dusty clothes.

"Why, it's Saturday."

Only Saturday? We hadn't even been gone a week! It seemed like a lifetime.

12

At Bay

July 1791 – June 1792

Now we were watched more closely than ever before, and guards followed Papa, Maman and Charles everywhere they went. They even watched them sleep! At least I was spared that. I was neither King nor Queen nor heir to the throne, so I didn't matter. I was glad of it!

One day in late September, Pauline returned. She came rushing in unannounced, so eager that she forgot her fine manners.

I sprang up and hugged her. "Oh, Pauline, it seems like a miracle to see you again. You can't imagine how I've missed you!"

"Perhaps as much as I've missed you!" said Pauline gaily. Then her face clouded and she said, "But think how terrible I felt, being so far away when so much was happening to all of you!"

"Oh, I'm glad, so glad that you didn't have to

go through all that." I stood back for a moment and looked at her. "But just look at you. Why, you're *fat!*"

Pauline chuckled. "Too much bread and cake and cream. I began to feel like one of the poor geese they were fattening up for Christmas. My sisters simply wouldn't let me leave the table until I was positively groaning. Orders from Maman, no doubt!"

We sat down, holding hands, just happy to be able to gaze at one another again.

A week later Pauline and I were curled up in our window seat with the draperies drawn when Papa and Maman and Tante Babet came in. I was just about to poke my head between the curtains to say that we were there, when a fierce argument broke out. Losing my nerve, I glanced at Pauline. To eavesdrop was bad enough for me, but far worse for her. As the voices rose in pitch, she turned pale. I squeezed her hand. After all, what could we do? We had already heard too much.

Maman's voice was trembling with rage. "I can't believe the Assembly can behave so badly. They show no respect for you, Louis. Imagine, Babet – when he visited the Assembly the deputies all just stood there with their hats on!"

Tante Babet's voice was cold. "What do you expect of revolutionaries? Yet you yourself deal with some of them, Antoinette," she said.

"Pah!" Maman said in disgust. "You know perfectly well that I despise all revolutionaries, Babet. Deputies in the Assembly, ranting lawyers, the press – all of them. True, I try to bring Barnave and a few other moderates around to our side, and I forward their letters to the Emperor, as they ask me to do. Why not? But you may be sure that I send secret instructions to the Austrian ambassador in Belgium. I tell him to ignore everything the revolutionaries say and urge the Emperor to send troops as soon as possible!"

"It could cost you your head if the revolutionaries discover what you're up to," my aunt retorted. "And I don't believe the Emperor is going to rescue us. He's only too happy to have a weak and divided France on his doorstep!"

"At least what I'm doing doesn't risk civil war, Babet," Maman snapped. "You should think twice about encouraging the mad schemes of your brothers. Now that they're safe abroad, what do they care if we're in peril? If they start a rebellion here, we'll be the first to suffer for it. And then the rest of France will go up in flames!"

Papa's voice was weary. "Please, my dears! Our situation is quite bad enough without our making it worse by quarrelling among ourselves like this. Antoinette, you know I don't approve of your trying to make fools of the deputies. It's terribly dangerous."

"Louis, I – "

His tone hardened. "I know you are trying to help me, but it won't work! And as for you, Babet, you must make it clear to our *dear* brothers that I'm still King of France and it's much too soon for either of them to try to step into my shoes!"

"That's unfair. No one could be more loyal to your interests than they are!" Tante Babet retorted.

"Listen to me, both of you!" Papa's patience sounded worn thin. "I've sworn to accept this Constitution, and that is what I shall do. If it doesn't work well – and I don't think it will – why then, the Assembly will have to change it, won't they? Meanwhile, I want no foreign invasions or civil wars on my behalf. Never shall it be said that the blood of Frenchmen was shed through my fault!"

Tante Babet must have fled the room then, because we heard silken skirts hissing like a basket of serpents, followed by the slam of a door.

"You too, Antoinette," Papa warned Maman. "Remember what I say, and don't do anything foolish,"

"If you refuse to act for yourself, you must expect others to act for you!" she said stubbornly.

We heard the rustle of her skirts followed by Papa's heavy tread. Then the door opened and shut again, and we were alone.

Poor Pauline sat with her eyes cast down, her cheeks scarlet with embarrassment.

"I suppose you thought that kings and queens and princesses never lost their tempers, did you?" I asked. "Knowing me should have taught you better than that! We're only too human under all our etiquette."

She gave me a watery smile.

116

"Never mind," I went on. "Even grown-ups can't be grown-up all the time. Anyway, now you know what it was like for me when you weren't around!"

❦ ❦ ❦

It was a bitter winter, and by spring Paris buzzed with rumours of war. The news criers bellowed constantly under the palace windows. The Emperor of Austria was about to declare war on France! France was about to declare war on Austria! The King's brothers were marching on the borders with a huge foreign army! The King had told his brothers to do no such thing, and all was well.

All anyone knew for certain was that *nobody* knew for certain.

At last, in April, the Assembly – eager to get in the first blow – insisted that my father declare war on Austria.

"But Louis, it's madness," cried my mother in despair.

"Of course it is," replied Papa gloomily. "But the Assembly will have it, though I've warned them of the risks. People will rejoice until France loses a battle. Then we must beware."

He was right, for soon the French army was being defeated in battle after battle, and the newspapers cried treachery. They accused my mother of betraying military secrets to Austria.

Had she done it? Day after day, she still wrote letters. I gazed at her weary face with a sinking heart, because I knew she *might* have done it. If there were no guilty secrets, why did she write everything in code? Why did she have to meddle? I asked myself. Though I already knew the answer – she was terribly afraid.

She had good reason. One morning, coming into a sitting room Maman often used, I noticed a large sheet of paper draped across one of our work tables. When I saw what it was, I stared in horror.

It was a large, coloured cartoon of my mother. She was depicted as a harpy with long razor claws, a forked tail and fangs dripping blood.

But that was not the worst. No. Poor Maman was shown without any clothes, embracing two figures labelled "The Enemies of France." The large title at the bottom read, "The Harlot of Austria Entertains the Enemies of the People."

I dropped the filthy thing as if it had scorched my fingers. I knew what a harlot was. I understood what that evil drawing meant, in all its ugliness.

And someone had left it there for Maman to find! Someone with access to our quarters. It had to be one of the guards or servants closest to us. I shuddered, and imagined gloating eyes waiting to delight in my mother's reaction. I felt surrounded by an invisible web of hate.

No one else must see it! I would cheat whoever had done this thing. I seized the drawing, rolled it up tightly and crammed it into the little enamelled stove in the corner. I stood watching the flames devour it. Then I sat down and cried. There was no one I could share this sorrow with, no one at all.

I did my best to hide it, but my face must have betrayed me, for Pauline kept asking me if anything was troubling me. I told her No, quite sharply the last time, and after that she didn't ask again. I noticed she kept avoiding my eyes too, and at last I began to wonder whether it was because I had been cross. I couldn't bear for anything to come between us.

"Now it's my turn to ask you if something is wrong, Pauline," I said to her one day, putting my hand on her arm. "Is it because I've been bearish lately? If so, I'm sorry to have grieved you."

"Oh, no. Not at all," she replied, forcing a smile.

"What, then?" I asked. "I know you too well now, you see. You can't fool me with your calm manner."

She dropped her gaze. There *was* something. I knew there was.

"I thought you trusted me," I said reproachfully.

Tears sprang to her eyes. "You know I do!" she said. "But . . . but I don't want to hurt you."

What could be the matter? After all, didn't I know worse things than she did? Unless . . .

"It's Sophie, isn't it?" I demanded. "You've had a letter. One you don't want to share." I held out my hand. "You know you don't have to show it to me. But if it's making us both unhappy, isn't it better if you do?"

"Are you *sure* you want to read it?" she asked. "Her words are . . . well, disturbing."

"Aren't they always?" I said. "Still, why not read it? Can it be worse than what people shout under our windows?" Or leave lying about our rooms? I added to myself.

Dear Pauline, Sophie wrote,

I was so disappointed to hear of your return to the Tuileries. It was such a joy to hear you were well away at last from all danger, and safe in the country with your sisters. For those whose hearts are with the people, these are splendid days in Paris. But royalists indeed have cause to tremble.

I must confess, Pauline, that sometimes I begin to doubt you, because you choose to live among those who are the greatest enemies of the people. Yet I know how kind and good you really are. I beg you to banish the royalist cause from your heart. Ask your mother for permission to return to the country. How happy that would make me, and all my family too.

Sophie was trying to persuade Pauline to leave! I glanced up, worried, but Pauline's smile and the little shake of her head gave me all the answer I needed. She wouldn't listen to Sophie – I knew she wouldn't! I went back to the letter.

Speaking of my family, have I told you that my youngest brother, Étienne, is now a captain in the National Army? We are all very proud of him, though of course we are terribly worried too. Now that your precious cowardly King has declared war at long last, the world will soon see what the armies of the Revolution can do. We will tear down all the other tyrannies of Europe and share the glories of democracy with nations everywhere!

My brother Pierre writes almost every day about the excitement in the Assembly. The King has no friends there anymore, because he vetoes new laws he doesn't like. Of course, everyone knows the Queen puts him up to it! Pierre says that the city is in a ferment of patriotism. Scarcely a day passes without some wonderful new event.

Yesterday Papa read me an article from one of the Paris papers. It seems an old friend of his, a Dr. Joseph Guillotin, has invented a new device to carry out the people's justice. It's a heavy, sharp blade mounted on a tall frame, with a chopping block fixed below. The criminal is bound in place on the block, then the blade is loosed. It falls with incredible force on the criminal's neck, and – voilà – the head is sliced off instantly. It is supposed to be much less painful than beheading or hanging, so it is humane as well as efficient.

Pierre writes that he saw it with his own eyes on April 25 last. The execution was very swift, and the crowd that attended was much pleased. Pierre thinks this new national razor will encourage people to obey the law, and it will be easier to dispatch criminals and traitors to the Revolution. By the way, the machine is to be *called the guillotine, in honour of its inventor.*

I looked up. Pauline's eyes were downcast. No wonder she hadn't wanted to share this letter. I was sorry I'd asked to see it, but now that I'd read this far . . .

Do not think my interest in this is bloodthirsty, my dear Pauline. You surely know me too well for that. You must understand, though, that the guillotine is a symbol of the glorious new world that is rising from the ashes of the old. We already have a new national Church and a new State. Even the calendar is to be new – did you know? It will begin with Year I of the Revolution, and so the dead past will be done away with entirely. And all titles are done away with, too. Everyone is Citizen or Citizeness. And don't think that because you were born a noble we can't be on the same side. Why, the King's own cousin, the Duc d'Orleans, has been a leader of the Revolution all along, Pierre says.

These are such exciting times, Pauline. Soon, I hope, even you will come to see that the future is on the side of the people, not kings. How I long for that day! Until then, I remain your true friend,

Citizeness Sophie Duvernier

I handed the letter back quickly, because my hands were shaking so much. Trying to hide my anguish from Pauline, I turned and rested my forehead against the windowpane. I closed my eyes, but saw only the colour of blood. Sophie was so sure of the future, so confident. And it was a future with no place in it for Papa or any of us. They had a fine new way to kill people now, too. I imagined a gleaming blade falling, heads rolling . . . And there, right below me, was a crowd shouting, "Death to the King! Kill the Queen!"

🐦 🐦 🐦

"Can it really be a year since Varennes?" I asked.

Tante Babet and I were standing at the south windows of the palace, watching an armed crowd strutting back and forth below. "Yes, a year," she replied with a sigh. "And even if we could forget it, why, here are the good people of Paris come to remind us."

"Tremble, tyrant, the people have risen!" chanted the crowd. Other voices shrieked, "Down with Monsieur and Madame Veto!"

I shivered. "Will they never leave us in peace?" I asked. For it seemed to me that despite all the fine talk of rights, only those who thought as the revolutionaries did had any rights at all.

We ate our midday meal to the sound of insults, but by three in the afternoon the crowd seemed to be breaking up. Then suddenly we heard the sound of hammering and of rending metal, followed by the pounding of many feet.

"What in heaven's name?" began Papa, but at that moment one of his gentlemen rushed in.

"Sire," he gasped, "the crowd has forced the gates of the courtyard. They're coming up the main staircase. They have pikes, axes!"

Ushers sprang to slam and bolt the doors into the

royal apartments, but Papa was too quick for them. He leapt through the doors to confront the rioters, with Tante Babet at his heels. Maman and I ran after them, but Pauline and the Duchess held us back.

The doors were made fast, and the crowd began to hammer on the other side.

Sick with horror, we waited. Over the roar of the crowd we could hear fearsome crashes and thuds. A gentleman ran in shouting, "They've brought a cannon up the main staircase to the landing! And I couldn't see His Majesty or Her Highness!"

"Mon dieu, Louis and Babet will be torn limb from limb or blown to pieces!" Maman sobbed wildly.

"No, Maman, no! God will surely protect them!" I cried, putting my arms around her.

My mother wiped her eyes. "You're right, Mousseline," she replied unsteadily. "We must trust to God. Only He can help us now."

The doors trembled under the blows of axes. We turned and ran until we reached a dead end. It was the Council Chamber, which was occupied by some of the National Guardsmen.

"I bring you the Dauphin of France, my good men," cried Maman. "I claim your duty to protect him!"

The soldiers placed Maman and me behind a heavy table, with Charles seated on it in front of us, then they surrounded us. The Duchess, Pauline and the others clustered behind. Not a minute too soon, for the crowd was upon us!

For a moment, the rough-looking figures in the

doorway simply stared at us in silence. Then they made a rush toward the table. The soldiers presented arms, and when the crowd saw they meant to use their weapons, the people fell back, muttering to themselves. Then a burly revolutionary stepped forward and said in a wheedling tone, "Come, sirs, no need to threaten us. We mean them no harm. The people have just come to look upon the Queen and her children."

He was lying. I knew it. If they had only come to look, then why had they chased us with pikes and axes? No, it was only the fear of the soldiers' bullets that had kept them from cutting our throats, I told myself, shuddering.

The man formed the crowd into a line that passed along the far side of the table, each person pausing a moment to peer closely into our faces. Some mouthed curses at us. Others simply scowled. One woman leaned across and yanked a red liberty cap down over Charles's head. Another brandished tricolour cockades under our noses.

"Take one, Mousseline," Maman said under her breath. "Pin it in your hair." She did the same.

Hour after hour we stood there. I tried to hold myself as proudly as my mother, but at last I began to droop. As if from far away, I heard a woman ask Maman how old I was.

"Old enough to suffer from an experience such as this," she replied.

A few moments later Maman gasped. I looked up,

and there was Tante Babet, walking along in the procession, a red liberty cap pulled down about her ears!

"Shhh!" she said, as she drew near us. "Don't let them see that you know me. Louis is safe. This is the only way I could let you know. Don't lose heart. The mayor has come, and perhaps this will soon be over." Then she disappeared into the crowd.

It was eight o'clock before the last of the rioters withdrew from the palace, leaving behind them a trail of smashed glass and woodwork. As soon as Papa came to join us Maman threw herself into his arms. He held her with one arm, and with the other reached out and drew Charles and me close to him.

"Now, now. It's over. It was touch and go for a few moments, but the soldiers had me climb on a window seat so people could see me. That seemed to make them calm down."

"I can't bear to think that you were in such danger without me beside you!" wept Maman.

"Your duty was to be with the children," Papa said. "Besides, I had Babet, and she's as good as any grenadier. She stood in the other window and stared right back at them!" He turned to smile proudly at my aunt. "Why, when someone asked if she was the Queen, she told them she was," he went on.

My mother stared blankly at my aunt for a moment, tears still streaming down her face. Then she said tremulously, "But . . . but Babet, that was horribly dangerous. You know how the people hate me. Why did you risk your life like that – for me!"

Tante Babet blushed. "I thought . . . the children need you more than they need me," she said. "And if it gained a little time, kept the mob from pursuing all of you . . . "

"*Mon dieu*, Babet!" cried Maman. She held out her arms and Tante Babet ran into them. They clung together, sobbing.

Sometimes, I thought, wiping my own tears, grown-ups did act like grown-ups.

Later, before I slept, I whispered into the darkness, "Please, oh please. Help me be brave like Tante Babet."

13

Shipwreck

July – August 1792

Like the survivors of a shipwreck, we could scarcely believe we were still alive. Every room in the palace showed the fury of the crowd, and we all knew that the rage smouldered on. All Paris waited, through the thundery heat of July. New troops arrived from the south, and they entered the city to the strains of a new marching song called the "Marseillaise." Soon harsh voices were singing it under our windows.

To arms, Citizens!
Form your battalions!
Let the blood of tyrants enrich our fields!

Just listening to it made me shudder. Would the terror never end? The grown-ups spoke little, but their grim faces said much. They too were waiting, I knew. Simply waiting.

Then, on the evening of the ninth of August, we heard that the people were arming themselves once again. The troops loyal to Papa gathered inside the palace gates, which were then locked. In the early hours of the morning the church bells began to ring. Not the friendly chimes that summon people to mass, but a harsh clanging, the signal to the mobs to gather.

They were coming again.

One by one my family came to gather in the large chamber overlooking the Seine. A fiery red dawn came up over the city, turning the river to blood. At six o'clock my father went downstairs to rally the National Guard. He returned ashen-faced. Some of the Guardsmen had jeered at him and turned their cannons around to face the palace.

"We can't count on their loyalty," he said heavily. "Only my Swiss Guards and my gentlemen-in-waiting stand between us and the crowd."

Two ushers set about dividing the fire tongs in half so that each would have a makeshift weapon. Pauline and I darted glances at each other. It was horrible, yet almost funny at the same time.

At seven o'clock a tall, grave-looking man arrived. Papa spoke quietly with him for a few minutes, then came over to us.

"The attorney general wants us to seek refuge with the Assembly, where we will be safe," he said. "The National Guard can no longer guarantee our safety here."

Maman's temper blazed up white-hot. "No!" she cried. "Shall we let this rabble drive us from our home? I would rather be nailed to the wall than run away from them!"

Papa shook his head. "Antoinette, we must think of the children, not of our pride," he reproached her.

Maman bowed her head. "It's true, we must think of them, and of all these others," she said after a moment, glancing around at our friends.

"Only our family may come with us to the Assembly," said Papa sorrowfully. "They'll allow Louise too, because she is a distant cousin. And Madame de Tourzel. I have been assured that the rest of the people here will be safe enough once the crowd knows that we have left."

I tugged at my father's sleeve. "Papa," I whispered, "when you said immediate family, you meant Pauline too, of course."

Papa looked down at me sadly. "My dear, it is not allowed. Madame de Tourzel is Governess to the Children of France. Her sworn duty requires her to accompany Charles and you wherever you go. This the Assembly understands and will permit. But there will be no other exceptions."

"But, Papa, we can't! We can't take the Duchess with us and make her leave Pauline behind! It's inhuman!" I cried.

My father turned away to move among the white-faced crowd of courtiers doomed to be left behind. He spoke gently to them, attempting to reassure them.

How can Papa *do* this thing? How *can* he? I thought wildly. Was Maman right after all? Wouldn't it be better to stand our ground here and die together than to abandon our friends?

As my father made his farewells, gentlemen bowed and kissed his hand, and ladies sank into graceful curtsies. There were many tears, but no protests. Not one word of reproach.

How could he bear it? I couldn't. Their courage and loyalty were heart-breaking.

Where was Pauline? Then I saw her and the Duchess standing close together in a corner. They said only a few words. Then Madame de Tourzel kissed Pauline gravely on the forehead, and after a final embrace, went to help Maman with Charles.

I went over and put my arms around Pauline. I could feel her trembling.

She tried to pass her fear off with a joke. "Now I'm jelly outside as well as inside," she said shakily.

I tried to comfort her. "Papa says it will be all right, that there will be no danger once the crowd knows we've left the palace. Then you can get away safely."

Pauline's dark eyes gazed steadily into mine. "Yes, I'm sure it will be so," she said. "And then, as soon as I can, I'll rejoin you. I've told Maman I want to. She told me to go to a friend of hers here in the city, and then to my sisters in the country. But I won't go away. I promise you!"

"Oh, I can't *bear* this!" I cried. I had tried so hard to be brave, but now I began to sob, and so did Pauline. I hugged her once more, and then I had to leave her.

Our little family group filed down the stairs and out into the palace gardens. The attorney general stalked solemnly ahead, glancing warningly to left and right at the jeering crowd that surrounded us. Next went my father and mother, then the Duchess, holding Charles by the hand. It was so hot that the leaves had fallen off the trees, and lay thick upon the ground. Charles scuffed his feet noisily through them.

Tears still streamed down my face as I walked beside Tante Babet. If people thought I was afraid for myself, well, let them!

The National Assembly was meeting in a building on the other side of the garden. We entered a dark outer passage and stood for what seemed like forever. Would the Assembly turn us back after all?

At last we were led into the glaring light of the crowded chamber.

Papa stepped forward and spoke to the President of the Assembly. "I come here, sir, to prevent a great crime," he said with simple dignity.

Dazzled by the sudden brightness of the chamber, I shielded my eyes with my hand and stared about me. The hall was packed to the roof with people, some standing, some leaning on railings, some slouching in their seats. They were all shouting at each other. It was like a roomful of parrots.

A guard led us to a kind of barred cage just behind the president's chair. Charles was fascinated. "Maman, what is this cage for? Are there animals here?" he wanted to know.

"Hush, Your Highness," whispered Madame de Tourzel. "There are no animals. This cage is where the reporter for the Assembly usually sits, so he can hear everything that is said and write it down."

The Duchess is right and wrong, I thought. Now there *are* animals in the cage. Us.

Sounds of gunfire came from the Tuileries. Someone shouted that the mob had broken into the palace and the Swiss Guard were firing on them. Madame de Tourzel turned white and swayed in her seat, and Charles began to cry. I was sick with fear. Was Pauline caught in a bloody battle between a mob out of control, and armed and desperate soldiers?

Minutes passed. At last one of the palace servants slipped through the milling crowd, and came close enough to whisper through the bars, "The ladies are safely away, Sire. They fled before the fighting broke out."

"Oh, my poor Pauline!" Charles sobbed. "Where are you, where are you?"

Now people rushed in shouting that the Tuileries was on fire, and the Swiss Guard were marching to the Assembly to try to help the King. Papa at once sent a note forbidding the soldiers to attack the crowd, and urging them to lay down their arms.

Minutes later, we heard screaming outside, so terrible I clapped my hands over my ears.

A deputy rushed out to investigate, and came back white-faced. "The Swiss Guard surrendered as ordered," he reported. "The mob is slaughtering them because . . . because earlier, the Guard fired on them!"

133

Papa slumped in his chair, and Maman held Charles tighter.

Now rough-looking men bearing loot from the palace forced their way into the Assembly. Maman turned her head away as sacred objects from the royal chapel and familiar things from her own bed chamber were waved under her eyes, to a chorus of insults.

We sat frozen, while waves of noise broke over us. *How much they hate us,* I thought dully, too numb to feel fresh pain.

It was evening before we were allowed to stumble off to hastily-made beds in the cells of the abandoned monastery next door.

Papa tried to cheer us up. "No guards, no servants," he said. "This is the very first time in my life that I shall sleep alone in a room. I may find it a great luxury."

Casting him a glance of reproach, Maman turned away to the dirty little room she and I were to share. I followed, my heart sore. How *could* Papa joke when we weren't really sure if Pauline was safe?

But the very next afternoon, a slender cloaked figure appeared outside our room in the convent and peered in hesitantly. "Madame? Your Majesty?" It was Pauline. Behind her stood Madame de Tourzel, her expression grave.

"Oh, Pauline! Thank heaven you're safe," I cried, jumping up and hugging her. Charles clung about her waist, and the three of us wept for joy.

"Maman doesn't want me to come back now,"

announced Pauline, with a triumphant smile. "But I told her that if she didn't let me come with you wherever you go I'd just run after your carriage through the streets of Paris. So she gave in!"

Maman kissed Pauline on the forehead. "Your mother is right to fear for you, especially after all you must have gone through. But how can I forbid you to come?" she said. "You see, my children simply can't do without you."

"The truth is that none of us can," added Papa, who had come up behind them. So he did care! I smiled at him, just a little, for the first time in two days.

At six o'clock our carriage rolled out into the twisted maze of the old city. Darkness fell before we reached our destination, the Temple. The front part of the Temple was a palace that used to belong to Oncle Charles. But behind it was an ancient tower with turrets and battlements, all that was left of a medieval castle. Once it had been a prison, and then it had held archives. And now . . . The palace was lit up as though for a festival. Light blazed out from every window and from torches set into its walls. Guards holding more lighted torches surrounded us, as we were led through the palace and into an inner court-yard. Beyond it loomed the grim turrets of the ancient Tower.

Across the courtyard we went, stumbling over the uneven cobblestones, and through a low wicket gate in the flank of the Tower. A twisting staircase made of thick slabs of stone rose up into the darkness above us. A guard bearing a torch climbed up first to light our way.

Noticing Maman's terrified expression, the Marseillais soldiers standing watch over us mocked us with the words of an old song: "Madame ascends her tower, Not knowing when she'll descend!"

Angry tears sprang to my eyes. How cruel they were! Trying to close my ears to their mockery, I rushed up the steps as fast as I could, stumbling on my skirts in my haste. Coarse laughter followed me. At the top I found my parents staring about them, stunned.

We were in a cramped apartment in a small turret of the Tower – just two small chambers with a little room between. Papa turned to the official who was with us. "But, Monsieur," he protested, "it must be plain to you that we cannot all fit into these rooms. We are too many!"

The man flushed. "Sire, you misunderstand. There is another such chamber above for you and your . . ." His voice trailed off in embarrassment.

"My jailers," said Papa.

"So only the ladies and children must stay here," the man rushed on. "And, Sire, Madame," he added, turning to include Maman, "you'll keep these apartments only until better ones can be prepared in the main part of the Tower."

"Let us hope that will be soon," said Maman, her nostrils flaring in disgust at the choking smells of dirt and damp.

Papa said goodnight and tramped upstairs with his guards and his valet. The rest of us settled ourselves as best we could, exclaiming over the dirtiness of the rooms. Poor Louise, who was terrified of spiders, shivered as she brushed away cobwebs from the corner she would have to sleep in.

I lay awake for a long time beside my mother in the hot, stuffy darkness. What did it all mean? Would Papa no longer be King of France at all?

What did people do with a king they no longer wanted?

14

One Day at a Time

August– September 1792

Two days later, just after we had eaten supper, officers from the government tramped up the stairs. They announced that everyone except our immediate family had to leave at once for La Force, a prison in another part of the city.

Pauline and I clung together.

"Surely these few friends may be left with us!" Papa protested. "What harm can they possibly do?"

"Our orders are to remove them," the officer in charge replied stubbornly. Then, perhaps softened by our tears, he added, "Come now, they'll be quite safe. Who knows? You may soon be allowed to be together again."

As Pauline and I drew apart, I felt a small hard object pressed into my hand. It was a wooden top that

Pauline had had in her pocket when she fled the Tuileries. We had played with it with Charles only yesterday, and Pauline had joked that it was the only possession she had left in the world. Now it was all she had to give. I closed my fingers around it, unable to say a word. With a backward glance, she followed the others down the stairs.

I sat down on the edge of my bed and buried my face in my hands. "How can I bear it?" I asked Tante Babet.

She sat down beside me and stroked my hair. "Try to take one day at a time, Mousseline. Just one day at a time."

Despite our heartache, we had to worry about how we could survive. How would we get food, or prepare it? Luckily, Cléry, one of Papa's valets, was allowed to return to him the next day. And a lad named Turgy, who had been with us at the Tuileries, offered to work as a cook and footman. So we had at least two faithful people about us.

And so we set about making a new life for ourselves. Papa seemed resigned to what had happened, almost at peace now that there was nothing more he could do. There was a small library in his room upstairs, and he set himelf to read every book in it, often staying up far into the night. He took to wearing his spectacles, which he'd always refused to wear in front of people before. Maman said they made him look like a shopkeeper.

Papa also brought some of the books down to use

for my lessons and Charles's. It was wonderful how clear he made everything. We drew maps and discussed the places on them. And we studied the history of France. I found out that kings have ruled our country for over a thousand years. What I wanted to know, though, was if Papa would be the last of them. But I was afraid to ask. France had a new government and constitution now, and hadn't Sophie's brother said the King would have to go? Did that mean that Charles would never be king after Papa?

One stiflingly hot day, Papa and I were doing lessons while Maman was lying down with a headache. Tante Babet was busy with Charles. Here at last was my chance. I didn't know how to begin, so I finally just blurted out, "Papa, will you go on being king now?"

The moment I spoke, I wished I'd curbed my tongue.

Papa looked up, startled, from the map he was drawing, and blinked at me in his near-sighted way. I could see that he was much moved.

"Forgive me, Papa," I said quickly, hating myself. "It's just . . . I've thought and tried to understand things. But now . . ."

He reached over and patted my hand clumsily. "No, Mousseline, it is your right to ask. You are old enough now, after all. Nearly fourteen. Almost grown up."

He took off his spectacles and polished them on his handkerchief. Then he went on, "And after all, it is because of me that we are here." He glanced around the shabby little room and sighed.

"That isn't your fault!" I said. "It's those wicked revolutionaries who have done it!"

Papa raised his eyebrows. "Why, Mousseline, don't you know *I'm* the one who started the Revolution?" he said.

"What, you?" I stared at him with my mouth open.

The guard, who had been dozing over his musket, raised his head and glared at me.

"Shhh!" said Papa. "Keep your voice down, Mousseline. Yes, me. Because I summoned the Estates-General. The country's finances were in ruins, you see. We had spent too much money, and something had to be done."

"Was it . . . was it all Maman's jewels and dresses? And her friends?" I whispered.

The corner of Papa's mouth twitched. "No, my child," he said. Then his voice became grave again as he went on. "It was more than that. Much more. We helped the United States against England in their War of Independence, you know. That cost us dearly. But the real problem was that France was an old piece of machinery that wasn't working anymore."

He stared down at the map of France we'd been working on, as if remembering all that had gone wrong. Then he went on. "I tried to fix it, truly I did. But nothing worked. So I called the Estates-General to grant new taxes on the nobility and the Church."

"Hadn't they paid taxes before?"

"No, and the people saw that as unfair. I thought

the new taxes would ease the people's grievances, and give us the money we needed to reduce our country's debts. But then people started to demand all sorts of other changes. It wasn't long before radicals were claiming that power belongs to the people and that a king has no rights at all."

He sighed. "I didn't mean things to go so far, of course. After all, I had a duty to defend the rights and powers I inherited from our ancestors, and hoped to pass to Charles someday. If some of those rights had to be given up, I wanted to do so freely, for the good of the country, to help make France prosperous again. But I didn't do the right things. It was hard to know what the right thing *was* most of the time. And it all got out of control so quickly."

He rubbed his eyes. "Do you know, Mousseline," he went on, "that there's one thing I fear above all else?"

I was surprised. "You, Papa? I thought you weren't afraid of anything."

He smiled. "Well, not most things. Not for myself. But I do fear making speeches. I haven't the gift of convincing people to follow me. I stammer and get tongue-tied and forget what I was going to say. So I stay silent instead, and that causes great problems. If I had been better at explaining things, and convincing people of what needed to be done, perhaps we wouldn't be here."

I thought about that. I wasn't much good at talking to people either, and always seemed to say the wrong thing. Then I asked, "But now, Papa? What will happen now?"

Papa glanced up to make sure the guard wasn't listening. "Mousseline, you must try to understand what I am going to tell you," he said, holding my eyes with his. "Charles is too young, so you must remember this, and tell him."

He gathered his thoughts for a moment, then said slowly, "I believe now that we can never undo the Revolution, never go back to the past. It is too late for that. We must go forward, or all will be lost, for us and for France."

I frowned, trying to understand. "You mean you have to accept this new government, and work with it?" I asked, puzzled. How could a king be a king if he couldn't do as he pleased?

Papa nodded. "That is called a constitutional monarchy," he said. "Oh, I didn't start out wanting any such thing. I inherited the right to rule from our ancestors, after all. And their power came from God, not from any constitution created by politicians!"

There was an edge to his voice as he said the words. Then he shook his head. "Over these last two years, though, I have come to see that the world is changing, and a constitutional monarchy is the only way to combine the best of the old with the new. But now is not the right time. The people's minds are inflamed with the Revolution, and they think it is the answer to all their needs. But one day they will see that it doesn't have easy answers to their problems either, and they will turn to the monarchy again."

I thought of all we had gone through in the last few weeks. The people's rage at us. Their hatred. It was hard to believe what Papa was saying.

"Truly, Papa?" I asked.

"Truly, my child. What we have to do is wait, and be ready to learn from the past and go on. Can you remember this, and tell it to Charles some day?"

"Yes. But you can tell him yourself later, can't you? When he's old enough to understand?"

Papa smiled. "Indeed, Mousseline, I pray I may be able to do so," he said quietly. "But if for some reason I can't tell him, swear to me that *you* will. This is something I can trust you alone to do. Not your mother. Not even your Tante Babet."

I knew there was some hidden meaning in what he had said, something I didn't understand. All the same, I was proud that he trusted me. I said, "I swear, Papa."

"That's my brave girl!"

Never before had I felt so close, so dear to him. My eyes brimmed with tears. Papa felt the moment too, for he blew his nose vigorously before he put his spectacles back on. Then he said, "Now, back to your lessons, or your mother will scold us for being slackers!"

❦ ❦ ❦

Just when we thought no more could happen to us, officers arrived the next day to take away Papa's sword. They even searched his pockets!

"You'll no longer be addressed as Your Majesty or Sire," one of them told him. "From now on you're simply Citizen Louis Capet, no different from anyone else."

Papa blinked at them. He'd whipped his spectacles into his pocket when he heard them coming up the stairs. "But why Capet?" he asked. "The Capets were a royal family that died out centuries ago. My own family name is Bourbon."

The officer shrugged. After that, some of guards in the Tower made a point of addressing my father simply as "Louis," with no last name at all. He managed to put up with this treatment somehow, but I hated it. They had taken everything away from Papa. Must they steal his name too?

On September second, noise began to filter through the thick walls of our prison. Then the dreaded tocsin bells began to clang from a nearby church. Cléry, who had gone to the market, rushed in, saying that rioters were gathering at La Force and other prisons in the city where political prisoners were held. My heart leaped into my throat. Pauline and our other friends were in La Force! What was happening to them?

For the last few days we'd been allowed to go out once a day to stroll in the Temple garden. Tante Babet and I usually played games with Charles, while Papa and Maman strolled back and forth under the trees, stopping now and then to chat with some of the guards or workmen.

But that afternoon, as we filed outside, the workers on the walls hurled insults at us.

"Austrian witch!" one man screamed at Maman, shaking his fist. "I'd like to knock your head off!" Another man aimed a shower of stones at Papa.

"Let's go back," my mother said, her face set. Only Tante Babet hung back as we turned toward the Tower.

"I'm trying to make something out," she said. "Over there in one of the houses above the wall – a woman is holding up a placard with writing on it!"

"Don't read it, Babet," Papa said. "It's sure to be something dreadful."

"No!" she cried. "It says that the armies of the Allies have invaded France. Already they've captured the fortress of Verdun. Soon they'll be on the road to Paris!"

"So that's what's causing the commotion in the city," said Papa. "I've dreaded such an invasion for years. It will harm France and inflame the cause of the Revolution. Still, I suppose we must hope the news is true. It's our only chance of rescue."

An angry official soon arrived in our chambers. He shook his fist at Papa. "You, Louis Capet," he said. "You will be the very first to die if the enemy reaches Paris!"

Charles shrieked and ran sobbing into the next room, where he threw himself face down on the bed. I ran after him and tried to comfort him.

But I needed comforting myself. I was so afraid for Papa. And Pauline – the crowds were attacking La Force, and she might be in even more danger than we were!

Early the next morning, an official told us that Pauline and the Duchess and Louise were still in La Force. "But I assure you that they're perfectly well and in no danger," he added.

"Thank God for that," breathed Maman. For we could tell from the noise outside that the city was still in an uproar.

The morning hours wore away. By the time we sat down to dinner at one-thirty, the distant noise had grown to a frightful clamour. After we ate we all went into Maman's room, while Cléry and Turgy went downstairs for their own meal.

Maman paced back and forth, wringing her hands. The noise was growing every minute. Amidst the din we could clearly hear Maman's name being shouted, mixed with cries and curses.

"Come, Antoinette. I challenge you to a game of trictrac," said my father.

Clever Papa, I thought. I knew he didn't care for the game.

Maman frowned, but she sat down at the table.

Papa and I exchanged a glance.

"Come, Charles," I said, drawing up two stools beside the table. "I think these players could use some advice. You help Maman, and I'll coach Papa."

Charles hopped happily onto the stool beside Maman. "Maman and I will trounce you easily, won't we, Maman?" he said. "Papa doesn't know a thing about this game, and neither does Mousseline."

My mother smiled faintly, and the game began. My idea had worked.

Despite Charles's boast, the game was a close one. We almost managed to forget the noise outside. Then shouts and screams burst out right beneath our windows.

"Some of the crowd must have broken into the garden," Papa said, getting to his feet.

"Please God we're better guarded here than we were in the Tuileries," said Tante Babet.

Maman said nothing, but sat biting her lips.

Our guard ran out of the room. Moments passed, then Cléry came in. He said nothing, but stood stiffly by the door, a look of horror on his face. At last he managed to say, "Your Majesties, whatever you may be asked, do not go to the window."

"Cléry, what on earth – " Papa began, but before he could finish our guards appeared, followed by four officers. The guards locked and bolted the doors behind them, then went at once to the window and drew the curtains.

One of the officers, tall and hard-faced, came to stand before us. "As you have no doubt guessed," he sneered, "the people of Paris have entered the grounds of the Temple. They wish the Queen to show herself at the window, perhaps just to assure themselves that she is still here." He turned to my mother. "I advise you to do so, Madame, lest they take it into their heads to come up here to see you instead."

Maman stared at him, then half-rose from her chair.

"No!" cried one of our guards. He was a decent young fellow and Maman had often chatted to him about his family. "No, Madame, don't go! They . . . It – " he broke off in a half-strangled sob. A low mutter of agreement came from our other guards.

"Idiots!" The tall officer glared at them, then swung around again to face my mother. "Very well, Madame, these fools are trying to hide something from you. The people have brought the head of Louise de Lamballe on a pike. That is how we take our revenge on tyrants!"

Maman rose to her feet, her face frozen with horror. Then, without a sound, she collapsed in a faint.

Papa and Tante Babet sprang forward to lift her. I ran for the smelling salts. Removing the glass stopper, I passed the bottle gently back and forth under Maman's nose. Tante Babet chafed her wrists. After a few moments, my mother's eyelids fluttered and she gazed up at us, her eyes filled with sorrow, and a terrible despair.

"Take her into Babet's room. It has no windows," Papa said. We half-led, half-carried Maman into the inner chamber. But she refused to lie down. Wrapping her arms about herself as if she were cold, she stood up stiff and straight. We begged her to speak to us, but she wouldn't utter a word.

At last the noise of the crowd began to die down, and the beating of drums and cries of command announced that reinforcements had arrived. As the Tower became quiet, Maman went into her own room and closed the door behind her. Only then did she begin to sob.

That night, I lay awake for hours. My eyes burned from weeping. I couldn't get out of my mind the words I had overheard the young guard whisper to another man as we tended my mother. "That head . . . The eyes wide open, staring! Her curls floating about her bloody neck . . . "

I buried my face in my pillow, trying to blot out the dreadful image. Poor Louise! She had been a foolish creature, always afraid of the least little thing. And now she had died horribly, alone and afraid. I knew the people had reason to hate her, but did anyone deserve such a death? Surely nobody could!

And where was Pauline tonight? Was she still in this world, or had she and her mother also been dragged from their cells and torn apart by the mob? Reaching under the pillow, I pulled out the little wooden top and pressed it against my cheek.

At last I slept, but only to dream of bloodstained golden curls floating on the breeze, and of Pauline stretching out her arms to me across a dark chasm neither of us could cross.

15

Fortune's Wheel

September – December 1792

"**W**hat's wrong with Turgy?" I said to Tante Babet. Every time our guard looked away, Turgy, who was serving us dinner, touched his fingers to his face in a very odd way.

"Shhh, Mousseline!" she said sharply, giving me a warning glance.

What had I done *now*?

Later, down in the garden, she drew me aside. "Never let on that you notice anything odd about Turgy," she said. "He and I have worked out a code of gestures so he can pass news to us while he serves dinner."

Trust Tante Babet to have a plan. "What was he telling you today?" I whispered.

"There will be another battle between the French army and the invading Allies. If the Allies win, we may be rescued."

"Will the battle be soon?"

"Yes, soon. Now listen closely, Mousseline. You must help me watch for Turgy's signals. That way, your mother and I can distract the guard if he seems to notice anything. You don't have to know the meaning of everything Turgy does, just remember exactly *what* he does."

"But how do I know what to look for?"

"The code is simple. His right hand always signals good news and his left, bad news. He may rub his eye, or stroke his hair, or touch his ear. The signal we watch for above all is if he touches the fingers of his right hand to his mouth. That means the Allies have been victorious and are fewer than fifteen leagues from Paris. Can you remember all this, Mousseline? It may be terribly important."

"You can depend on me, Tante Babet."

One of the guards strolled past, glancing suspiciously at us from under his bushy brows. Tante Babet pretended to adjust the frill on my cap. "Good girl!" she said. "One more thing. Don't mention this to Charles. He's still too young to understand how serious it is, and he might betray us without meaning to."

On September twentieth, the bells of Paris began to ring out joyously. Our guards grinned and clapped each other on the shoulder. We didn't need Turgy's signal to tell us that the great battle had been won by the French army. The invaders were in full retreat toward the frontier.

Tison, one of our jailers, soon arrived to gloat.

"Thanks to the glorious army of France, the assassins you paid to murder honest Frenchmen have been defeated," he sneered. "You'd better beware, Louis. The Revolution knows how to deal out justice to its enemies!"

The next afternoon, drums rolled outside the tower and then a proclamation was read out. My father was no longer king. No one was. France had become a republic.

Our guards stared at us, openly curious. My parents and Tante Babet were too proud to show their grief. I struggled to keep my tell-tale face from showing mine. We had nothing left now but our pride.

🍂 🍂 🍂

In the new apartment, the deep windows that pierced the thick stone walls of the Tower had iron bars across them. Each one was also blocked by a curious kind of shutter fixed to the outside wall, angling steeply outward to block the view of the ground below.

In the bedroom Maman and I would share, I stood on tiptoe looking up at a bronze clock on the mantel. The clock face was surrounded by a wheel bearing small figures of people. Beside the wheel stood the figure of a woman, who pointed to the wheel and its passengers with an enigmatic smile.

"What a funny-looking clock," I said. "Who's the woman meant to be, Tante Babet?"

"The goddess Fortune, Mousseline. Her wheel bears the figures of mankind. Some rise upward to fortune, others go down to ruin," she replied. Then she added, "No doubt we're supposed to reflect on that."

We settled in. To Maman's sorrow, the government decreed that Charles must now live downstairs with Papa. So now we were all together only at mealtimes, and for walks in the garden.

One day we returned from our walk to find a crude drawing of a guillotine and a severed head chalked on the wall of the passage. Below it was written: The King gets a shave from the national razor!

Charles read it aloud, then burst into tears.

Papa calmly wiped the drawing and words away with his handkerchief. "It's a pity to frighten children with such things," he said, looking at the guards reproachfully. A few of the younger ones had the grace to look ashamed.

In early December, we learned that Papa was going to be put on trial. Then the guards made a sweep of all the rooms. All sharp objects, even table knives and sewing scissors, were forbidden from now on. By quick thinking, I saved a little pair of embroidery scissors. A small victory, but I relished it.

At dinner, looking at a roast chicken he was supposed to carve without a knife, Papa said, "What a coward they must think me to be – as though I'd end my troubles with a carving knife!"

"Papa!" I cried.

Seeing the stricken looks on our faces, he apologized for his clumsy joke.

On December eleventh, Charles appeared in our

rooms after breakfast, and ran straight to Maman.

"Why, Charles! What a happy surprise!" she cried, holding out her arms.

I glanced at Tante Babet, who returned my look soberly. Something was wrong. He was never allowed to be alone with us now.

"Where is your papa, Charles?" Tante Babet asked him.

"Downstairs. He had to go out somewhere. He said I should come upstairs and have my lessons with you. And the guards let me," said Charles cheerfully.

The happy smile froze on my mother's face.

Soon afterward we heard drums beating and the sound of troops clashing their weapons in the courtyard.

"He's going on trial," whispered Maman.

"Come, Charles," I said quickly. "It's past time for our lessons. We mustn't shirk or Papa won't be pleased with us." I held out my hand.

Charles gazed at me gravely for a moment, then followed me to the table. I settled him beside me with a map he could fill in. But he stopped now and then to look over worriedly at Maman. I felt a stab of pity for him. He was beginning to understand how terribly wrong everything was.

The long day crept by. At last Cléry came with a message. My father would be tried for his life on a charge of treason to the French nation. During the trial, he wouldn't be allowed to meet us or exchange messages with any of us.

"Oh, cruel, cruel," my mother murmured, wringing her hands. "But tell him, Cléry, that our hearts are with him."

Cléry bowed deeply. "He knows, Your Majesty, but I'll surely tell him."

🌿 🌿 🌿

Each day my mother begged the guards to let her have newspapers so we could follow Papa's trial. They always refused. But we must have had some friends left, for every day a news crier stationed himself right under the Tower walls and cried out the latest headlines. Surely someone must have paid him to do it.

Looking at my mother's strained face as we stood listening in the dusk, I suddenly realized, Maman is old! She was thin, and haggard, her hair completely grey now. I felt cheated of something, almost angry at her. How could she change when I needed her to stay the same?

Days passed, and still we heard the sounds of my father's escort arriving in the morning and returning at night.

"How long must this go on?" Maman said one dark afternoon. "Do you think they've even allowed him a lawyer? He must be exhausted. How can he possibly defend himself?"

"I don't think it will matter what Louis pleads in his defense," Tante Babet replied quietly.

My mother rounded on her. "How can you be so cold-blooded, Babet!" she demanded.

For a moment Tante Babet's eyes flashed, but then she placed her hand on Maman's shoulder. "Not cold-blooded, Antoinette. But I'm afraid we must prepare for – "

Just then the clashing of keys and the grating of locks announced the changing of the guard, and the conversation ended.

Prepared for what? I wondered. The new Republic of France had taken everything away from Papa. Surely it wouldn't take away his life too.

16

Into the Dark

December 19, 1792– January 21, 1793

December nineteenth was my fourteenth birthday. As he cleared the dinner table, Turgy dropped a platter of meat and gravy right beside me. The guard shouted at him, and in the confusion that followed I felt something pushed against my foot.

"A thousand pardons, Madame," said Turgy. He bent down to clean up the mess, while the guard cursed him for his clumsiness.

I glanced down at him. Turgy's eyes were sparkling with amusement. It must be a ruse! And what was against my foot?

It was a small parcel. I hid it under my apron and slipped off to the bedroom as soon as I could. It was an almanac for the year 1793, and inside was concealed a loving message from Papa.

Slowly I turned over the pages. The almanac had been printed in the new style of the Republic, but my father had patiently gone over every page, writing in the festivals, the round of court rituals, and the saints' days of the old religious calendar. He must have done it night after night in the few moments left to him after he returned from his trial.

Tears ran down my cheeks and splashed onto the almanac, blurring the ink. I blotted the precious pages with my handkerchief, and tucked my present away under my mattress.

The next day it was Tante Babet's turn to receive something smuggled in by Turgy – a ball of string, much knotted. When the guard's back was turned she whisked it into her pocket.

What on earth would Tante Babet want with a ball of string? I wondered. I soon found out. It was a way to communicate with Papa on the floor below.

That night Tante Babet lowered the string, and back up came a small scrap of paper with a message pricked on it in code. My mother's hands shook as she smoothed out the message and tried to read it by the light of our bedroom candle.

"He's well," she breathed. "He thinks the trial will be over before long. He has lawyers, and he hasn't given up hope that the verdict may go in his favour. He sends us all his love."

A forlorn Christmas came and went, and after it, New Year's Day. And then, the trial was over. Tante Babet and Turgy had worked out a new code of signs. From this, we learned that January eighteenth was the day on which the verdict would be made public.

From Tante Babet's trembling hands the knotted string was lowered that night, and a message drawn up. My mother read it, then covered her face with her hands. "All is lost," she whispered. "He has been found guilty, and they have condemned him to death."

It – it couldn't be. They couldn't really kill Papa. Couldn't, couldn't, couldn't!

"Louis Capet will die!" screamed the news crier the next day. But no one came to tell us, and we were still not allowed to see my father.

My mother was in despair. "What kind of monsters are they?" she moaned. "Will they send him to his death without letting us even speak to him?"

At seven in the evening of January twentieth, the heavy tread of guards' footsteps on the stairs made us all leap to our feet. It was a message from the government. Papa was to be executed by guillotine the next day. They would allow us – allow! – to see him now.

Hurrying downstairs, we found Papa waiting for us in a little chamber off the guardroom. He looked terribly weary. His heavy features were lined, and his eyes had dark circles under them.

"Come, my dears," he said, holding out his arms. Weeping, Maman and Tante Babet embraced him, then sat down on either side of him. He gathered Charles and me into his arms. Charles sobbed bitterly. I tried hard not to cry, but couldn't help myself. My father's eyes were full of tears too, as he patted us awkwardly.

He stood Charles between his knees, and put one arm around me as I knelt beside him.

"My poor Louis," cried Maman. "How much thinner you look!"

"Now, Antoinette, you know that must be an improvement." Papa tried to manage a smile.

"Oh, how *can* you joke, Louis! I can't bear this, I *can't!*" she wept, throwing her arms around him and sobbing. Tante Babet, choking back her own sobs, sat by helplessly.

"Let me tell you how it was," Papa said at last. He told us all that had happened at his trial, and how he and his counsel had prepared his defense.

"We did well, even though the prosecuting lawyers tried to say that some letters I wrote to Mirabeau were treasonous. It was nonsense, of course. I was only trying to find a way to regain some of the influence I had lost. All in all, I think at least some of the deputies believed that I wasn't plotting against the nation, but many were afraid to vote in my favour. I was found guilty. When it came to my sentence, though, many of them risked their own safety to vote against the death penalty, and it was very close." He sighed. "I was condemned by just one vote. It was the Duc d'Orléans, my own cousin, who cast it."

Horrified, I remembered how Sophie had written that Papa's cousin was a leader of the Revolution.

"Oh, the monster!" cried Maman.

"Yes, he calls himself Philippe Egalité now, the people's friend," said Tante Babet bitterly. "May his precious people serve him as treacherously as he has served you, my brother."

"We must forgive him, Babet," Papa replied. "I have no time to bear grudges now. And some good will come of my death, for they've promised me that all of you will soon be set free."

Papa placed both hands on Charles's shoulders. "My son," he said, "You understand that I must leave you all tomorrow. You must be brave, and look after your mother and sister and aunt."

Charles nodded, tears rolling silently down his cheeks.

"And I want you to swear before God, Charles, that you will never in any way seek revenge on those who have condemned me. Swear now, lift up your hand like this."

Charles raised his hand. "I swear, Papa."

"That's my brave boy. Love God, and if it ever comes to you to rule France, as I believe it will, do your best to be a good king and a friend to your people."

Then Papa turned to me. "And you, Mousseline, you must be brave too. Your mother and aunt will need you more than ever now, and you must be a guardian to Charles." Looking deep into my eyes, he added "And above all, remember . . . our history lesson."

"I will, Papa," I sobbed.

At ten o'clock he got up. We all clung to him, begging for just a few more minutes. But he put us from him. "I must go now and prepare myself for tomorrow," he said. "I must make my peace with God."

"But we will surely see you again tomorrow?" pleaded Maman.

Papa hesitated, then said, "Very well, at eight o'clock."

"Oh, why not at seven?" she cried.

"Well, yes, at seven."

I flung myself on Papa and clung to him. I just couldn't let go. I buried my face in the cloth of his coat, and breathed in his familiar smell of soap and wool. I felt his big hand smooth my hair.

"Goodbye, my Mousseline," I heard him say in a muffled voice. Then he tore himself from my arms and hurried from the room.

I screamed, and fell on the floor.

"Get up, child. This does no good," said Tante Babet, bending over me.

But I couldn't. She had to half-carry me up the stairs.

None of us slept that night. As the slow-footed hours crept by, I could hear Maman comforting Charles, who would doze only to wake, crying and terrified, from unspeakable nightmares. Beside me, the steady click of Tante Babet's rosary in the darkness measured her prayers for Papa.

I could find no such comfort. My heart was stony cold. God wanted Papa to die, or He wouldn't let this happen. I wouldn't pray to such a God.

Instead I lay trying not to think about what was going to happen to Papa. But I couldn't help it. I kept hearing Sophie's words about the guillotine over and over in my head. Would Papa be terribly afraid? Would he feel its razor-sharp blade slice through his neck? Would it hurt horribly? I turned over on my stomach and buried my face in the pillow, sickened by my own thoughts.

We rose long before the first grey light of morning crept through the shutters. The fires were not yet lit, and the rooms were very cold. The bells of a nearby church struck six, and soon after we heard the sound of footsteps on the stairs.

"Please God," murmured my mother, "they have allowed him to come to us earlier than seven."

But it was only a guard, who had been sent to borrow a prayer book for Papa.

Seven o'clock struck, then eight. I realized the truth before any of the others did. I had guessed it all along. He wasn't going to come. He never intended to. He couldn't bear to go through saying goodbye again, because it would have made him weak when he needed to be brave to die in front of the people.

Still we sat, frozen in our places, hoping against hope for a final glimpse of him. At nine we heard drums and the tramp of marching feet. Orders were shouted. We strained our ears listening for the sound of footsteps going down the stairs, but heard nothing. Then there came the clatter of iron-shod wheels on cobblestones as a carriage drove away.

At the sound, Charles raced to the door and pounded on it with his fists. "Let me out! Let me out!" he cried.

"For what purpose, my young sir?" asked the guard.

"To tell the people that my father is a good man, and they must not kill him!"

Tante Babet picked Charles up and carried him, sobbing and struggling, to a sofa.

Maman gave no sign that she had heard any of this. As if in a trance, she rose and moved slowly toward the west window. I knew she was following in her imagination, as I was, the route of the carriage through the streets of Paris, and down toward the river to the Place de la Révolution where the guillotine waited on its bloodstained scaffold. When she reached the wall, she stood with her hands clasped so tightly to her breast that I could see the knuckles stand out white.

I ached to comfort her, and to be comforted. "Maman?" I said. I tried to put my arms around her. She gave not the slightest sign that she knew I was there.

"Leave her be, Mousseline," said Tante Babet in a low voice. "She can't hear you now."

And so I stood alone, each passing moment more agonizing than the last. There was a tiny bit of blue sky visible at the top of the shutter. Such a tender pale blue, as if it didn't belong above such an ugly world.

The bells struck ten, and then, moments later, we heard the boom of artillery, and the faint echo of cheering from across the city. It was done. Papa was dead.

Maman now roused from her trance and moved across the room to Charles. Raising him to his feet, she drew him fiercely against her for a moment. Then she sank to the floor in front of him in a most profound curtsey.

"The King is dead," she said in a high clear voice. "Long Live the King!"

17

One by One

January 1793 – May 1794

Somehow, we went on living. Our existence was like the embroidery I hated. Little by little, stitch by painful stitch, we were making a new, smaller pattern for our lives.

It was hard to think of Charles as the King. But my mother insisted that we pay him the formal respect that was due to him, and she gave him Papa's position of honour at the head of the table. Charles took it all with grave dignity.

Now that the worst had happened, nobody seemed to worry as much about us. Two friendly guards, Toulan and Joubert, brought us newspapers, and talked to us a little. And so we gained a little news, a little hope.

Then Joubert came on duty one day looking pale and shaken. "All is lost," he said bitterly. "Tison saw Toulan hand you a newspaper. He has denounced us, saying that we plotted your escape."

We never saw him again. Late the next evening, new guards appeared and grimly turned our rooms upside down.

Then Charles fell ill. He was feverish and his head ached, and he had a pain in his side. A prison doctor came and in time Charles began to get better. But the doctor warned that lack of exercise was endangering his health.

"He must get well, he *must*," whispered my mother. She watched every night by his bedside, refusing to let us help her.

One evening in early July, I was reading to Maman and Tante Babet while they sewed. Charles had already gone to sleep. About ten o'clock we heard the tramp of feet on the stairs, then the clashing of locks and bolts as guards threw open the double doors. In a loud voice, an officer read a decree. Charles Capet, it said, was to be removed from his mother. He was to be lodged separately in the Tower, and placed under the guardianship of a tutor.

"No!" cried Maman. "No, you can't, you mustn't. He's only eight, just a baby. And he has been so ill!" Charles woke up and flung himself, sobbing, into her arms.

"I have my orders," the officer said. He turned to the men behind him. "Take the boy," he said harshly. "Lodge him below."

Deadly pale, Maman thrust Charles behind her, and faced the guards. "I won't let him go. You'll have to kill me first!"

"That, Madame, would not be a bad thing for France," growled the officer. "But tell me, do you feel the same about the lives of these other ladies? If you make a struggle, they'll surely be harmed. And so may the boy."

Defeated, Maman turned to Charles. "You must go, my son. I can't prevent it. Be a good boy – " her voice broke " – and . . . and don't forget to say your prayers and bless Papa."

"Maman, Maman, I don't want to leave you!" sobbed Charles, flinging his arms tightly around her waist. One of the guards reached for him, but he ducked away and ran back to kiss me and Tante Babet before they caught him. He looked very small as he was led away between two guards.

"Oh, my little king," whispered Maman. "May Louis's spirit watch over you!"

Charles cried for two days. White-faced, we sat listening as the sound of his sobs drifted up through cracks in the wooden floor. Later, there were worse things to hear. Curses, the sound of blows, and terrified whimpering from Charles.

"Mon dieu, they're going to murder him," sobbed Maman.

"They wouldn't dare," said Tante Babet. "Even in this benighted country it would be too cruel to kill a child!"

A week dragged by. One morning we heard Charles's voice, thin and high, singing a song.

"What is it? What's he singing?" I asked.

"It's the 'Carmagnole,' " Tante Babet hissed. "One

of the most bloodthirsty revolutionary songs. I can imagine what kind of tutor they've given him!"

Beneath us, the thin voice piped on and on. It faltered, then picked up again, repeating. There came the sound of a blow. The voice sang on, pitiful as the cry of a trapped sparrow. Day after day we listened, fearful of what we might hear, but more frightened if we heard nothing. One day we heard Charles laughing shrilly, and the sound of bottles clinking. In high, silly tones, his little voice was mouthing curses. Coarse voices roared out, urging it on.

"They've given him wine," said Maman dully. "To make him do things he wouldn't want to. May his health withstand it." Each time our guards appeared she confronted them, begging that we might be allowed to see Charles.

"Why, the lad's getting a proper revolutionary education. You wouldn't want to interrupt that, now would you?" said one fellow mockingly.

Now the guards came in only to bring our meals and check the windows. As if we had hacksaws to cut through the bars, and wings to fly away! Tante Babet and I looked after Maman. Most of the time she would forget to eat.

Then it came again in the dead of night – a thundering of feet on the stairs, a heavy pounding on the door.

When we drew back the inside bolt, we saw the same officer who had taken Charles. My mother drew back in horror.

"Widow Capet," he read out in a harsh voice, "you're to be taken to the prison of the Conciergerie, where you'll stay until your trial."

"Trial! What is she accused of?" Tante Babet exclaimed.

"The people will decide," replied the officer, stony-faced.

"Let me go with her," I said. "She needs someone to take care of her."

"And I, too," pleaded my aunt.

"My orders are only for the Widow Capet. You must both stay here," he replied.

Moving like someone in a dream, Maman finished dressing, while Tante Babet and I hurriedly parcelled up some things she would need.

Maman kissed me on the forehead. "Take courage, my child," she said. "May God comfort you. Obey your aunt in all things. She will be a second mother to you."

Unable to speak, I stood with tears streaming down my face.

My mother turned to Tante Babet, and her courage gave way. "Babet!" Maman cried bitterly, falling into my aunt's arms. "Oh, Babet, look after my children!"

"I will, Antoinette!"

Maman walked out into the antechamber. As she stepped through the low doorway leading to the staircase she struck her forehead sharply on the stone lintel. A guard asked her whether she had hurt herself.

"Oh, no," replied Maman, as she went down into the dark. "Nothing can hurt me now."

Day after day we hoped for a scrap of news about her. At last we heard from a guard that she was in solitary confinement. But she was well, and the turn-key's wife was kind to her.

Early in October, there was a bustle in the court-yard of the Tower. Moments later guards arrived and ordered me downstairs. Terrified, I hung back.

"I insist on going with this child wherever she goes," said Tante Babet.

"She's only going to the floor below," returned the guard. "She'll be back soon. Let her come along and make no fuss."

Fighting back fear, I followed them down to the second floor. There were the rooms where we had seen Papa for the last time. Tears welled into my eyes. Then, through an open door, I saw Charles sitting on the edge of his bed.

"Charles!" I cried. I rushed in and hugged him before the guards could stop me. "Oh, Charles! Are you well?" I asked him. "We think of you every day, and pray for you."

He was thin and pale, and he gazed at me dully at first, as if he scarcely knew who I was. Then his eyes lit up. "Mousseline! I – " He broke off and cowered away into a corner as the guard seized my shoulder and thrust me roughly into the next room.

"None of that. You're here to see these gentle-men," the guard muttered.

I found myself facing a group of men seated at a long table. One of them stood up and frowned at me.

"Thérèse Capet, here are some questions which I shall put to you in the name of the government. Answer them honestly," he said. He pointed to a hard wooden chair, and I sank onto it, trembling. Never in my life had I been alone with men, much less total strangers. I could scarcely hear past the pounding of my heart.

"Do you know Citizen Toulan?"

I swallowed. If I admitted I did, these men might punish him or my mother for it! "No, Monsieur," I said.

"What? You say that you don't know Toulan who was on guard in your rooms almost every day?"

"I – I don't know him well, no more than any of the other guards."

"Did you never notice your relatives talking more with Toulan than with any of the other guards?"

"No, Monsieur."

My questioner shot a suspicious glance at me from under his brows. Then he looked down at the pile of papers before him. "Very well, let's move on to another matter. We have here a statement sworn to by your brother, Charles Capet, under oath." He came around the table, holding out a large document with a heavy wax seal the colour of blood. "Do you agree that this is your brother's signature?"

It *did* look like Charles's childish scrawl. "Yes, I think so," I said.

"Your brother swears here that both your mother and your aunt have abused him, so much so that his health has suffered. Will you swear to that?"

"Abused? I don't understand . . ." The eyes of the men in the room seemed to bore into me. What did they mean? Sweat broke out on my forehead and I drew a shaky breath. "My mother and my aunt have always shown the greatest care for my brother. His welfare has always come first with them."

The questioner grew impatient. "Come, don't be sly. You haven't answered my question. Let me put it even more clearly. Your brother swears that both ladies on occasion took him into their beds." He peered at me. "Do you understand what that means?"

A blush seared my cheeks, and bitter bile welled into my throat. "That is infamy! Infamy!" I cried. "My mother and aunt did sometimes sleep with Charles when he was ill, but only to be there if he needed something. To suggest anything else is horrible!" I began to weep out of sheer disgust.

Mercifully, one of the other men took pity on me. "Come, Chaumette," he said. "It's clear she knows nothing about such matters. Ask your other questions."

The interrogation dragged on. They wanted to know about the flight to Varennes. Who had known, who had helped us? And later, had my mother or my aunt communicated with people outside the Tower, or outside of France? In a daze, I struggled to answer without saying something that could harm anybody.

After three endless hours, I was allowed to stumble back upstairs. They forbade me to speak to Tante Babet. We exchanged anguished glances as she was led down to be interrogated.

An hour later she returned, looking ill. We gazed at each other for a moment, then burst into tears.

"I couldn't have believed men could be so vile," Tante Babet wept, hugging me against her.

For a moment a flame of anger burned in me. "Charles – how *could* he? How *could* he accuse Maman and you of . . . of . . . "

"Hush now, hush," soothed Tante Babet. "You know how they've tormented him, Mousseline. He's terrified of the brutes. And you must remember he's too young to fully understand the evil of what he's saying. We must forgive him."

"Well, then I hate them for making him say such awful things. I hate them, I hate them all!" I cried.

"Now listen to me, Mousseline." My aunt gave me a little shake. "You must *not* hate them. Do you hear me?"

"They murdered Papa!" I said. "And they're cruel to Charles. And now they want to harm Maman. And you."

"I know. I don't ask you not to hate them for *their* sakes. It's for yourself, Mousseline."

"I don't understand," I sniffed, fumbling for my handkerchief.

"If you hate them, it will kill your soul. You'll become crabbed and twisted and ugly inside, just as some of them are. And never forget that even revolutionaries aren't all evil. Remember those who have tried to help us, and don't give in to hate."

I sighed. "I'll try. But I don't know if I can help it."

Tante Babet gave me a loving look. "Come, give yourself credit, Mousseline. You've done many hard things since this all began. I know you can do this too."

Day after day we strained our ears hoping to hear the news criers in the distance. At last came the words we had dreaded: "Widow Capet . . . Tried . . . Condemned!"

"Don't give up hope, Mousseline." Tante Babet tried to comfort me. "Your mother is an Austrian archduchess. They would be mad to harm her. Now they have condemned her publicly, they may even send her out of France, or keep her where she is."

"Or send her back to us?" I asked, though it seemed too much to hope.

And so we waited and prayed. Our plates and tableware were taken away now. They even took our bed sheets too, saying we might knot them into a rope and use it to escape. Our food was common prison fare – coarse bread, a bit of stringy beef once a day, a cup of thin soup. The guards left us entirely alone, week after week, only pushing our meals through the door on a tray.

"They mean to break our spirit," said Tante Babet, "but we won't let them. We must keep busy every single minute!"

So she set up a routine, a kind of ritual, that we followed religiously day after day. First we dressed and then smoothed down our beds. We dusted and swept the chamber until it was as neat as we could make it. Then we prayed, and after that took an hour of brisk exercise by walking to and fro. After our noon meal we read to each other from our few remaining books, and played trictrac. Later we mended our clothes and knitted.

I discovered I hated knitting as much as I'd ever hated embroidery. To make it even more stupid, we had to unravel our work when we were finished, and start over, because we weren't allowed any more wool.

And so the weary weeks passed. Then one night in the dead of winter, we were awakened by noises in Charles's chamber below. It sounded as though heavy boxes were being moved.

"Could they be taking Charles?" I whispered. After the bustle died away we put our ears to the floor, but could hear no sound from the chamber below.

"My brother, is he well? Is he still there?" I asked a guard the next day.

"He's well enough. Of course he's still there," the man grunted.

🍂 🍂 🍂

Spring came at last. One May evening we had gone to bed early because there was not enough light to read or sew by. Suddenly the bolts on the outer door were shot back and there was a pounding on the inner door. A guard shouted at us, demanding that we draw back the inside bolt.

"In a few moments," Tante Babet called back. "When we have dressed."

The pounding redoubled. When we were both ready, Tante Babet opened the door.

A large group of guards stood outside. "Citizeness, you will please come downstairs," the officer said to my aunt.

"And my niece? I do not wish to leave her."

"We'll attend to her later."

Tante Babet looked about for her cap. "Don't worry, Mousseline," she said. "It's probably only another interrogation. I'll be back soon."

"No, Citizeness, you will not be back," the officer growled. "Come at once."

Tante Babet embraced me. "Have courage, my dearest girl. Trust in God," she whispered. "And ask for a woman to stay here with you. You must not be alone here with men all about you. Do you understand? Promise that you will ask!"

"I promise, Tante Babet," I said.

"Enough delay!" Cursing, the officer seized Tante Babet by the arm and shoved her out of the room.

I saw her white dress glimmer down the dark staircase before the door was slammed shut in my face. I rested my forehead on the rough wood, pressing my palms flat against it, and listened with all my might. I heard the clash of muskets, the shouted orders, and then the rumble of carriage wheels over cobblestones.

"No," I said, to the darkness. "Oh, please, no." Little by little, I slid down the door until I lay huddled at the bottom of it.

18

Alone

May 1794 – June 1795

Hours later I awoke in the dark. Why was I on the floor? Then a cold tide of memory flooded over me. They had taken Tante Babet. I was alone.

I got stiffly to my feet and groped my way to the bed that had first been my mother's and then my aunt's. It was mine alone now. Wrapping myself in an old shawl of Maman's, I curled up and buried my face in the evil-smelling pillow. Anything was better than staring up into the dark.

The Tower was utterly silent. At that moment I would have welcomed the clink of a guard's sword belt or the rattle of a key in the door. I mumbled my prayers over and over, a numbing patter to keep me from thinking. At last I slept.

When I awakened it was morning, the sky clear and pale blue above the shutters. Shivering, I poured cold water into the basin and washed myself. Then I dressed hastily.

It seemed as though hours passed before the guards brought the tray with my breakfast. "Please," I cried, springing up as they opened the door. "Tell me, where is my aunt?"

The guard paused, then with a sideways glance at his companion and an odd little smirk, he said, "She has gone to take the air."

Take the air? What did he mean? I hesitated, then asked, "If my aunt can't stay here with me, may I please be taken to my mother?"

"We will speak of it," the same man replied over his shoulder as the door clashed shut behind them.

I tried to swallow a mouthful of bread, but it stuck in my throat. I forced down a sip from the bowl of milky coffee. What was going to happen to Tante Babet? Perhaps the government was going to send her out of France! Hadn't the guard said she had gone to take the air?

Just thinking about her made me feel so alone. My eyes filled with tears. Then I thought, Here I sit doing nothing. If Tante Babet were here, would she not reproach me? So I jumped up and made myself busy, sweeping and dusting, and smoothing the bed as she had taught me. Then I sprinkled the last of my water about to freshen the air. When there was nothing more I could do, I sat down to read one of Tante Babet's religious books. But though I tried my best, my thoughts raced so fast that the lines of print danced before my eyes.

If Tante Babet might be set free, what about my mother, and Charles, and me? After all, Papa had said they had promised him that we would all be set free. Perhaps Maman was already abroad, and had been for months. I shivered. No. That couldn't be. The people hated my mother so. They wouldn't set her free. But she might be in a different prison, might still be perfectly well, mightn't she?

And Charles? What of him? We had heard nothing from his room below for so long now. But the guards had said he was still there. And so . . . I made myself follow the thought through to the end. Charles was the rightful king of France. The Revolution would never, *could* never, let him go.

"And how could I leave him, even if they would let me?" I said aloud, gazing up at the little patch of blue above the shutters. "So then . . . " So then, must I live here alone all the rest of my life? I wanted to be brave, but the thought was too terrible. Burying my face in my hands, I wept.

When they brought my midday meal, I remembered my promise to Tante Babet. "Please," I said. "I need . . . May I have a woman to keep me company?"

"Perhaps. We'll think about it," came the answer. I knew what that meant.

They took away my penknife now, and my sewing scissors, and the little tinderbox I used to light fires to heat water for washing myself. Even my candles went.

Not long afterward, a stranger visited me, a narrow-faced cold-eyed man. The guards seemed as terrified of him as I was.

Snake! I thought, trying to hide my trembling. Too frightened to speak, I held out a letter I had written, which begged that I be allowed to see Charles. The man took it, but didn't trouble to read it. He just glanced around the room, including me with the furniture, and left.

The guards' eyes followed him as he disappeared down the stairs. "Robespierre," one said in an awed voice.

"How many heads have rolled on his orders, I wonder?" said another.

"Don't ask – unless you want yours to join them," replied the first.

Day after day I followed the same schedule of getting dressed, sweeping, dusting, reading, praying. I tried to work at an old piece of tapestry Maman had left behind, but gave up in despair. It was too hard for me. If only I'd paid more attention when my old macaw had tried to teach me! Then I picked up Tante Babet's knitting and struggled with it. As the evenings grew lighter, I tried to mend my one dress, for it was too short and too tight. But all I could make were a few crude patches.

Each day I walked for an hour back and forth across the room, holding Maman's little gold and amber watch in my hand. At first I paced numbly to and fro, while it ticked into the silence. But too many thoughts would come, and with them a cloud of fear that darkened my mind. So instead I murmured as I walked, a foolish little chant that matched itself to the rhythm of my steps.

I am Marie Thérèse Charlotte de France. Granddaughter of Maria Theresa, Empress of Austria. Daughter of Louis XVI, King of France and Marie Antoinette, Archduchess of Austria, Queen of France. Niece of Élisabeth, Princess of France. Sister of Charles, King of France.

And friend of Pauline.

Oh, Pauline!

No, I couldn't, I wouldn't think! But my free hand sought the little wooden top which I always carried in my pocket. Touching it, I marched on. Then, turning in the corner, I would begin my litany again.

I am Marie Thérèse Charlotte de France . . .

My dreams were haunted. One night I awoke to the echo of my own screams, and lay awake weeping until the first cold light crept through the shuttered windows. That morning, only my fear that the guards would force their way in if I didn't answer the door made me get up and drag on my clothes. I picked up a knitting needle and, not really knowing why I did it, scratched a message on the plaster wall of the chamber:

Marie Thérèse is the most unhappy person in the world.

Live, my good mother, whom I love so much but of whom I can hear no tidings.

O my father, watch over me from heaven!

Weeks passed, and in my despair I thought I no longer cared what they did with me. Yet my heart leaped with fear one July morning when I heard the rattle of drumbeats and the clang of the dreaded tocsin bells. Was a bloodthirsty mob coming to drag me out?

The guards clashed open my door, bringing my breakfast. They looked so grim that I was afraid to ask any questions.

Early the next morning, drums began to beat, and once again gates clanged open and shut. Boots thudded on the stairs, and I heard the bolts on the door of Charles's chamber below being shot back. I jumped out of bed and dressed with shaking fingers. I had scarcely finished before the bolts on the outer door of my own room were thrown back. Trembling, I went over and drew the inner bolt.

Outside was a group of officials decked out in colourful tricolour sashes and plumes.

"We have come to make sure you are safe and to inspect the conditions under which you live," their leader announced, staring at me.

After a quick look around, they clattered away down the stairs, but from behind my closed door I could hear them shouting at the guards to be loyal to the government.

"Down with Robespierre! Long Live the Republic! Long Live the Nation!" rough voices cried in answer.

I sank down, my heart beating wildly. The terrible Robespierre must have fallen from power, then. And . . . and they had stopped first at the floor below. That meant that Charles was still there, still alive! Oh, why hadn't I thought more quickly? Why hadn't I asked after him, begged, demanded?

Three days later, there was a polite rap at my door. I went to open it, wondering why it wasn't the usual pounding. Outside was a dark-haired young man and one of the guards.

"This is Commissioner Laurent," said the guard. "He has been newly appointed."

Now, what sort of creature is he? I wondered. Then I had it. A cat – a sleek cat with glossy black fur.

Laurent gazed at me kindly, and spoke in a soft voice. "Mademoiselle, it will be my pleasure to see to your needs," he said.

"And my brother's?" I croaked, scarcely daring to hope for an answer.

A shadow seemed to cross Laurent's face as he replied, "His especially."

"Oh, please, tell me – " I began as he turned away. But the guard slammed the door.

The next morning, Laurent appeared after breakfast. This time he was alone. Again he spoke to me politely, asking if there was anything I needed.

Cautiously, fearing a trap, I asked for my tinderbox and a candle.

He said I could have them! Growing bolder, I asked, "Charles . . . my brother . . . He is still here? He is well?"

"He lives, as you know, on the floor below yours," Laurent said. "I am expressly forbidden to tell you more, Mademoiselle."

"May I see him?" I begged. "I have asked so many times . . . "

"I will place your request before the Council of the Temple. I can do no more," he said.

"But my mother . . . My aunt, then?" I pleaded. "How are they?"

"Mademoiselle, please understand that I can never speak to you about any of your family. Pray don't ask me to," he said. Then he turned on his heel and left.

I was crushed. Even this gentle jailer wasn't really a friend after all. It had been foolish of me to hope.

Not long afteward, though, Laurent brought a new official, named Gomin, to meet me. He said Gomin would live with Charles in his room, and look after him. I searched the man's face for a clue to his character. His plain blunt features were almost ugly, but he had an air of honest kindness about him. A sturdy cart-horse, I thought.

I was glad Charles would have company now. But why, oh why, wouldn't they let me see him, even for a moment?

🍃 🍃 🍃

Autumn turned to winter. I had a small fire and candles now, and no longer had to go to bed as soon as it got dark. But the chamber was still freezingly cold and damp. Even wearing every layer of clothing I possessed, I still shivered, and my hands cracked and bled with chilblains.

As the weeks passed, it was as if the cold of the Tower seeped into my very soul. Numbly, I went through my daily tasks. What else was there to do? But when they were done I sat for hours, thinking of nothing. I didn't weep – I had no tears left.

I no longer murmured my little chant as I paced back and forth. What did it matter who I had been, whom I loved? They would never, ever let me see any of my family again.

I couldn't even hope for death to rescue me from my loneliness. They wouldn't kill me now, I told myself bitterly. They had buried me alive instead.

New Year's came and went. Laurent ordered some grey woollen stuff for a gown for me, and there were needles and thread and even some tea and orange water. I cared for none of it.

Then one day as I was passing through a doorway, my shawl snagged on a cut in the frame. I stooped to twitch it free – and then I saw words scrawled on the wall in Maman's uneven writing:

Charles, 4 feet

Thérèse, 4 feet, 8 inches

Of course! Maman had made two cuts in the door frame in the spring of 1793 to measure Charles's height against mine. Charles had been so proud, and crowed, "Hurry up and grow, Mousseline! I'll be taller than you soon!"

But my mark was so low – I must have grown!

The only mirror was over the mantel in my bed chamber. I had never thought of using it because, even on tiptoe, I had barely been able to peer over the mantel. Now I was level with the clock, with Fortune and her wheel.

I faced the mocking bronze smile of the goddess,

afraid to look beyond her. What a poor ghost or scarecrow I must be.

Summoning my courage, I peered into the mirror. Then, "Tante Babet!" I whispered. I reached out with my cracked fingertips to the reflected image, my breath misting the ice-cold glass. The lips of the reflection moved in response, and its fingertips touched mine. It was as if my dear, dear aunt had come back to comfort me. But it was not she. The reflection was my own.

Truly, I looked like Tante Babet. My hair had darkened to the same chestnut brown as hers, and I had the same round cheeks, the same high colour. But no, it wasn't all my aunt. For the eyes that gazed back at me were my mother's. And Papa was there, too. Something about my nose? My forehead?

Why, I've grown up – here! I thought, astonished.

"I'm alive," I said, into the listening silence. And so much more than alive, for the small me I remembered had somehow become this tall young woman, strong and well grown. Papa would have been so proud of me . . .

I drew my breath in sharply, stung by a piercing sense of shame. Oh, Papa! In my selfish misery, I had pushed his memory far away these many months. I had forgotten my promise to him!

Almost as if he spoke the words in my ear, I heard my father's voice saying, *If for some reason I can't tell him, swear to me that you will.*

Suddenly I understood the meaning behind the

words. Papa had thought all along that he would be put to death. Of course he had. And he had trusted me – me! – to give his message to Charles. Some day I must do it! We were alive, after all, and we could hope. I gazed fiercely into the mirror. I had Tante Babet's form. Now I must find her courage. At last I wept, and my tears were tears of life.

🍃 🍃 🍃

Spring came, and I was allowed to go up to the top of the Tower for exercise. I bounded up eagerly each day, hoping to catch a glimpse of Charles, though I never did.

A new commissioner, named Lasne, arrived and explained that he would be in charge of me from now on. He was a bushy-haired fellow, with a button nose and a big bristling moustache. He seemed friendly enough.

I puzzled over him for a moment. A walrus? No, an otter.

"I shall miss Monsieur Laurent," I said. "He was . . . kind."

"Now, don't you fret Mademoiselle," said Lasne. "I'm not a fine-looking fellow like Monsieur Laurent, but I'll do my best for you. And Gomin is very good to the lad downstairs."

"Thank you," I whispered, not daring to ask more. It was the first time in months that anyone had mentioned Charles.

Lasne kept his word. My food improved – a small dish of asparagus here, a joint of cold chicken there.

Another dress, too, and better shoes. When I thanked him, Lasne tugged his moustache and said, "Well, it's spring, after all, Mademoiselle. And things have begun to loosen up since Robespierre went to the guillotine. All sorts of things." And he winked.

So the terrible Robespierre was dead! Could it mean that the Revolution was coming to an end at last?

Sniffing the green smell of the wind from the top of the Tower, I could feel my spirit unfolding like a bud in the mild sunshine. But oh, how lonely I was! I ached for someone to talk to. So I screwed up my courage and asked Lasne for a woman to be my companion. Surely he wouldn't bring someone horrible – he was too kind.

Lasne rubbed his nose. "Well, Mademoiselle, I'll ask the Council. We'll see what they will do."

If they give me someone who isn't an absolute monster, I'm sure I couldn't help loving her now, I told myself.

Even the guards pitied my loneliness. As I paced back and forth on the top of the Tower they would sometimes whisper scraps of news about Charles.

"Not very well, he isn't," said one older man who looked as if he might be a father himself. "Poor lad. But he's getting the best of care."

"Thank God for that," I breathed. Each day now I fixed an anxious look on Lasne. He never said anything in so many words, but some days he would nod in the direction of the lower floor and smile. More often, though, my unspoken question would be answered by a sad look and a shake of the head.

One day in early June, Gomin appeared, carrying a small bundle of brown and white fur, and placed it in my arms.

"A puppy!" I cried, delighted.

"Monsieur Lasne said you might like to have him," Gomin said gruffly. "His master loved him dearly, but he had to go away."

"Oh, he's lovely!" I stroked the puppy's long, silky ears. "What sort of dog is he, Monsieur?"

Gomin scratched his head. "Don't know. I guess you might say he's all sorts, Mademoiselle," he replied. "Name's Coco."

"Coco, we're going to be great friends," I said, hugging the little dog tightly in my arms, feeling its warmth and the beating of its heart. "Thank you, Monsieur Gomin," I added, with tears in my eyes.

"I'm sure you're welcome, Mademoiselle," he said. He took out a large, none-too-clean handkerchief and blew his nose loudly.

Not many days later, I was reading near one of the windows, with Coco curled up on a cushion at my feet. I heard the door open, but didn't look up, thinking that it was only one of the guards on some errand. Then I heard a little noise, like a stifled sob, and looked up to find a pretty young woman gazing at me with tears running down her cheeks. She dropped awkwardly to her knees. Then, as if she had done something she wasn't supposed to, she scrambled to her feet.

"Mademoiselle," said the woman, "my name is Renée de Chanterenne. They . . . that is, the government, have sent me to be your companion. You won't be alone anymore."

19

False Dawn

June– August 1795

I didn't know what to say. She was so different from anything I could have expected. A fox, I thought, gazing at her delicate pointed face and reddish hair. She's a pretty fox.

The stranger repeated, "I'm Renée de Chanterenne. I've been sent to live with you as your companion. You *do* want a companion, Mademoiselle, don't you?"

"Yes! Oh, yes!" I managed to croak at last. "Tante Babet, I mean, the Princesse Élisabeth, always said I must have a woman to live with me after she went away. But when I asked, nothing came of it."

"Oh, but that was the past. Everything is so much . . . calmer . . . these days," said Madame de Chanterenne. "Believe me, the government's only concern now is to act in your best interests."

Could it be true? In the days that followed, my

doubts slowly faded. Who could feel gloomy with a companion who was so cheerful? Renette, for she insisted on being called Renette, clucked in disapproval over my rough red hands. Someone must be sent for at once to take over cleaning the chamber.

"And your poor voice! So rusty. It's from being all alone here, in the cold and the damp with no one to talk to!" she said indignantly.

"I can't blame the Tower for that, Renette," I confessed, smiling. "I've always had a voice like a crow." Such an old Sorrow! And such a small thing, it now seemed to me.

Was last year's grey dress already too tight, too short? There would be new gowns, and at once.

Soon she was unpacking morning robes of coloured taffeta, and delicate afternoon dresses of muslin. Grandest of all was a splendid gown of green silk, for special occasions. I stroked its shimmering folds, and rubbed them against my cheek. It was lovely, but . . . No *paniers*, I told myself mockingly. Never again. The new styles were slender and straight, with a very high waist.

My pretty fox tilted her head to one side, and gazed at me appraisingly. "It's the perfect colour for you, Mademoiselle," she said.

"It's beautiful," I agreed. "Do you know, I'd forgotten clothes can be a pleasure!"

Renette looked disappointed, so I added quickly, "But I do thank you for all these lovely things." I waved my hand at the silk shoes and stockings, the dainty underwear, the scarves and laces and caps that were spread out over the bed.

"*De rien*," said Renette. "I've barely begun."

And she was as good as her word. Would I like to study English? Italian? Notebooks and lexicons appeared on my table as if by magic. I liked to draw? Chalks, pencils, brushes and India ink rained down around me. And would I perhaps enjoy walking in the garden instead of just pacing to and fro on the top of the Tower?

Would I!

I could hardly believe my good luck the summer evening I first went downstairs, with Coco running ahead of me. The garden with its chestnut trees and simple flowers looked like paradise to me. Even the tops of the funny crooked houses that overhung the Tower's high stone walls seemed full of magic. People actually lived there, lived real lives, and laughed and cried and dreamed.

I took a great gulp of air, and seized my skirts in both hands. Oh, it would be good to run and feel the wind on my face again. But . . . but I was sixteen now. Too old for childish games. So I paced along the gravel path, watching the lights come on in the attics of the houses all around, and thinking about my family who had last walked here with me.

Soon I turned back to where Renette sat waiting under the chestnut trees. If only I could know how Maman and Tante Babet were, I thought, and get some news of Charles. For though Renette talked about everything else, she would not speak of my family. Nor had Lasne or Gomin given me any more clues about Charles's health.

"Are you tired already, Mademoiselle?" Renette asked, as I wandered up to her in the dusk.

"Not really, Renette. Just ... sad. I last walked here with my family, and I can never be at peace until I know how they are. God grant they may have found companions as kind as you."

My pretty fox dropped her eyes and bit her lip.

When we went down the next evening, Renette stopped short and gazed up at the top of the wall, with an angry expression on her face.

"What is it, Renette?" I asked. Then I saw it too. In the attic window of one of the houses overlooking the walls, a very tall man stood gazing down at us. As I looked up, he bowed deeply. Then he deliberately pulled at his right earlobe with his right hand.

It had to be a mockery of some sort. I dropped my eyes. But something about the gesture tugged at my memory. Then it was as if I heard Tante Babet's voice echoing back over time from this very place, this garden.

The right hand always signals good news.

The code! It was the old code of hand signals. But who could it be who knew them? It must be, had to be, someone who had been close to us. Someone so tall. Someone who bowed just so. Could ... could it be Hué, Papa's second valet? He had tried to stay with us in the Tower but had been sent away with Pauline and the others.

Again the man in the window tugged at his earlobe. What was the meaning? Be hopeful? No. Something about friends. *Friends are approaching!* That was it!

It was on the tip of my tongue to blurt everything out to Renette, but I stopped myself in time. She might report it to the government and Hué might be punished.

"It seems we have a visitor," Renette said coolly.

"What can he want?" Even to me the question sounded forced.

"Some royalist wanting to see his princess, I expect," said Renette. "Come, let us walk about. We must not let this intruder spoil your exercise."

Intruder! As we strolled along, I felt as if that cold word had opened up a gulf between the two of us. To me the visitor was someone who had known my family, even knew where they were now. But for Renette, he was an unwelcome intruder.

The next day the man was there again, and other people too. Men bowed, women curtsied and waved their handkerchiefs. Uncertain what to do, I nodded stiffly back, with a guilty sideways glance at Renette. The signal was repeated: *friends are approaching*. In the old days, it would have meant that the Allied armies were nearing Paris to rescue us. That couldn't be true now. So it must mean other friends. But who? Each day the crowd at the window grew larger. Other windows overlooking the walls were taken over too. The sound of a harp drifted down into the garden, and the sound of a voice singing a song I had never heard before:

Be calm, unhappy one,
These doors will open soon;
Soon from your chains set free,
'Neath radiant skies you'll be.
Yet when from this abode
Of grief you take the road
Remember that even there
True hearts made you their care.

My eyes filled with tears. People had been thinking of me all along, then. I hadn't been forgotten. Oh, how wrong I had been to sink into selfish despair!

But what about Charles? Why weren't they singing about him too? For a moment panic seized me, then I shrugged it off. The song surely meant nothing.

The crowds and serenades continued for almost two weeks. Lasne, Gomin and Renette grew daily more tight-lipped and anxious. Then one afternoon the windows above the garden were empty. I felt an odd sense of loss. I hadn't really enjoyed being viewed like a goldfish in a bowl, but I had felt comforted to see that so many people cared about me.

My fox was all smiles now. I smiled back, though I was quite sure that she or one of my other guardians had reported my visitors to the government.

Then, one morning in late August, Renette came into my room with a grave expression on her face. Sitting down and taking both my hands in hers, she said, "Mademoiselle, I know that there is a matter that lies between us, that prevents us from being true friends."

So she *had* stopped the visits!

I met her gaze steadily. "I didn't truly like to be on show that way," I said, "but, oh, to feel that people outside care about me, what happens to me – "

"I didn't mean the serenades."

What could it be, then? "Do . . . do you mean my wish to know about my family?" I faltered.

Renette nodded. "Yes, Mademoiselle. Before, I was forbidden to answer any questions about them. But Lasne, Gomin and I have told the Council of the Temple that you have a right to know. So ask what you wish. I am allowed to answer."

At last! "Oh, Renette, you can't imagine what this means to me," I gasped. "After so many months, to know . . . Dearest Renette, where is my mother?"

At first I didn't understand the shake of her head, the look in her eyes. Then she said, "Mademoiselle, you have no mother."

"No mother?" Of course I had a mother! Then I gasped, "You mean, she . . . they . . . ?"

"Yes, Mademoiselle. The Queen was guillotined nearly two years ago. In October, seventeen ninety-three."

"Maman . . . dead?" I felt as if my heart had turned to stone. All these months – years! – while I had clung to hope and prayed for her, my mother had been cold in her grave. It was as though a dark gulf had opened at my feet. She was gone. Forever. There would never be another chance to win her love, to show her mine. I began to tremble, then willed myself to stop. No. I must not let my despair master me. And there was still some hope. Tante Babet . . .

I forced myself to meet Renette's pitying gaze. "And . . . my aunt?" I asked.

"The Princess Élisabeth was guillotined on May tenth, seventeen ninety-four."

"Tante Babet too?" I felt faint, and clung to the arm of the chair. May tenth, May tenth, I thought to myself, dazed. That was the day after the guards had taken her away, the very day I had asked after her, hoping against hope she had been sent into exile.

She has gone to take the air.

The guard's mocking words sounded in my ears. I had not guessed mockery so cruel could exist in God's world.

Renette reached out to me, but I drew away. There was a long pause. Then, scarcely able to utter the words, I asked in a very small voice, "But Charles, my little brother. He's still here, isn't he? Right below me? Gomin used to tell me how he fared . . . "

Renette's eyes were glazed with tears. "Mademoiselle, my dearest Mademoiselle, your brother died of fever here in the Tower on ninth June last."

"Ninth June?" At that moment Coco, asleep on his cushion, whimpered in some dream. As I reached down to pat him my hand froze in midair. *Coco!* Gomin had brought him to me in early June, had said the little dog had been much loved but his master had to go away . . .

I picked Coco up, hugging his warm furriness

against me. Though I already knew the answer, I asked. "Coco was Charles's dog, wasn't he?"

Renette tried to speak, but couldn't. She just nodded, while tears trickled down her cheeks.

I had no questions left. I sat silent, clutching Coco. Then I sobbed once, a dry racking sob that pierced my chest like a blade. My eyes brimmed, then overflowed, and the room and Renette dissolved. I wept bitterly into Coco's fur. He whimpered and wriggled in my arms, trying to lick my tears away.

20

Friends

September 1795

The next morning I confronted Renette dry-eyed. "You've told me what I asked of you, Renette, and I thank you," I said. "But I must know everything – not only that they died but how it was with them at the end. Will you tell me that too?"

Renette nodded. "I'll tell you all I know, Mademoiselle, and Lasne and Gomin will tell you all they know, which is more."

And so, from the three of them, I learned it all. How my mother had gone to the guillotine in an open cart, reviled and insulted to the end by a furious crowd. How Tante Babet had comforted others condemned to be executed with her, and had died so bravely that the crowd fell silent, awed by her courage.

But Charles's fate, told me by a weeping Gomin, was the most terrible of all. It was true that he had died of a fever, as Renette had told me, and that he had been well cared-for in his last illness. But his death was really caused by what he had suffered the year before.

Gomin hung his head, telling me about it. "They left the poor child shut up in the dark, Mademoiselle. Simon, his jailer, left in the winter to take up a new position. After that, no one entered the lad's chamber. They just pushed food in through the door. His cell was never cleaned, nor his . . . his excrement removed. Nor his filthy clothing or bed-linen changed. They left him like that for six months. He sank into a stupor and made not a sound."

Tears of sorrow and anger spilled down my cheeks. "How could they be so cruel?"

Gomin shook his head. "Robespierre was in power then. He was a fanatic. He wanted your family dead. Every one of you. But even *he* didn't quite dare to execute children in public. So he tried to cause your deaths through neglect and illness. It wasn't until he and his followers fell from power that your brother's condition was discovered. Laurent told me later what he had found. He said it made him sick to see it – sick in body and in soul."

"Thank God for Laurent!"

"He did everything he could. He had your brother bathed and his cell cleaned, and he got him better food, something the boy could eat. Later, when I came, I was able to do even more. But it was too late. Your brother was never well again, and seemed damaged in his mind. Yet he was a dear little fellow,

Mademoiselle. He died in my arms." Gomin's ugly honest face was wet with tears.

I struggled to say what must be said. "Thank you for telling me, Monsieur Gomin," I said. "I had to know." Then I went back into my room, closing the door behind me. I knelt down in front of the little *prie-dieu* where Tante Babet had spent so many hours, and buried my face in my hands. I tried, but I couldn't pray. All I could think was, Why me? Oh, *mon dieu*, how can I still be alive when all the rest are dead?

What was I good for after all? Charles was lost with the rest of my family. All Papa's dearest hopes were betrayed – I could never deliver the message he had entrusted to me.

For many days I was like a sleepwalker, dead to those about me. Then, little by little, I let Renette coax me back to our studies and walks, though my heart was like lead within me. What else could I do, after all? If I sat and stared at the wall I would go mad.

So one bright September morning we were studying Italian when the door burst open, and a tall young woman with dark hair flew into the room. Renette stood up, frowning.

But before she could speak I cried, "Pauline! Oh, it's Pauline!" I threw myself into her arms, and we hugged, laughed, kissed and wept all at once. Then another visitor appeared. Out of breath from the steep climb, she leaned in the doorway for a moment. She was very stooped, with snow-white hair. At first I didn't know her. Then I did. It was the Duchess.

"Oh, Madame de Tourzel! Thank God you are alive too!" I cried.

"Your Royal Highness," murmured the Duchess. She sank to the floor in a deep curtsey. Blushing at her own forgetfulness, Pauline quickly did the same.

"Oh, don't! Please, don't!" I cried, holding out my hands to both of them. Not etiquette – not now! It was like acting a play I had once been part of, but no more.

"To see you again after . . . after all that has befallen," the Duchess murmured. She wiped away her tears. "You must forgive me, Madame. I am quite overcome."

I led her to a seat, then stood hand-in-hand with Pauline smiling down at her. "Now I understand what Hué was signalling to me. *You're* the friends who were coming!" I said.

"Just so. The government has relented at last." Madame de Tourzel cocked her head to one side, and gazed up at me. "But Your Highness, how fine and tall you've grown!" she exclaimed. "And you were such a tiny creature. Why, you're the living image of Madame Élisabeth. But like Their Majesties too."

"Oh, do you think so? I'm so glad! I thought it was so, I hoped it was!" I said eagerly. "That means so much to me . . . now." Then, reading the question in the Duchess's eyes, I added softly, "Don't be afraid. I know . . . all there is to know. Thanks to my good Renette and others who have told me the truth."

I brought Renette forward and introduced her to

my friends. Madame de Tourzel nodded pleasantly enough, but she gave Renette The Look. Renette flushed.

"Maman and I have been trying for months to be allowed to see you," Pauline said eagerly. "We received permission to come this very morning. Of course, we rushed here as fast as we could." She laughed and added, "I think I trampled on one of the guards, I was in such a hurry to get upstairs."

Renette offered to order some tea. The moment she had stepped out of the room, Madame de Tourzel reached into her pocket and drew out a much-folded letter. "Read it quickly, Madame," she urged. "Later, we must find a chance for you to write a reply."

The letter was from my uncle, Louis Stanislas, the Comte de Provence, and had been sent from Italy, where he lived in exile. My eyes raced hungrily over the page. *My dearest child . . . my love for you and my concern for your sufferings . . . must come to live with me if you are allowed to leave France . . .*

I looked up, my eyes full of tears. "Thank you for bringing this. It must be horribly dangerous for you to do it – I mean, if someone found out. But oh, it's so good to realize that I have *some* family left," I said. "Of course I must answer him!" But Renette returned with the tea-tray, so I couldn't right then.

We talked and talked.

"My heart breaks when I think of you left alone here month after month!" sobbed Pauline. "If only I could have been with you!"

"You're with me now," I replied, "and that matters more than you know." It was true: for the first time in many days, I felt alive again.

I put my hand in my pocket and pulled out the little wooden top Pauline had given me so long ago. I enclosed it in her hand with both of mine. "You see," I added, "I never forgot you for a moment. This has been with me through everything."

All too soon it was time for the Tourzels to leave. "I know you'll come back," I said shakily, as I hugged Pauline. "But I don't want to let you go."

"Don't worry," she replied. "I'll be back so often that you'll soon want to tell the guards to keep me out!"

That night, I sat down to write the first letter I had ever written to my friend.

My dear Pauline, I wrote,

The pleasure I felt at seeing you has done a great deal to lighten my sufferings. Even had I not known you and loved you as I did, the proofs of affection which you have given to my family and myself would have made me your friend for life. But I already loved you tenderly; and you may judge, therefore, how dear you are to me now. I love you, and shall never cease to love you all my life.

Written at the Tower of the Temple,
6th September, 1795.

Marie Thérèse Charlotte de France

21

Morning

September– December 1795

Pauline was as good as her word – I saw my friends often. The concerts and serenades from the attic rooms overlooking the garden began again too.

"When will it end?" I asked, as Pauline and I paced under the chestnut trees, listening to the music. "This was forbidden before, you know."

"Perhaps this time those who support you can't be sent away so easily," said Pauline, her eyes dancing. "Maman says people are growing tired of the Revolution. They may turn to the royalists again. Perhaps your uncle will be able to return as king. And, *voilà*, you will make a stately progress from the Tower back to the Tuileries."

"Only the Tower could make the Tuileries look good to me," I said, shaking my head. "Anyway, I can't believe it could happen. People hated us so, before. *You* know that, better than anybody!" I shivered.

Sensing how I felt, Pauline deftly turned the subject by pulling a letter out of her pocket.

"No! Don't tell me!" I exclaimed. "Not Citizeness Sophie – still alive, and writing!"

"She doesn't sign herself that way anymore," said Pauline. "Read for yourself."

And I did.

> My dearest Pauline:
>
> I thank you for your kind inquiries after the health of my family. Unfortunately, my poor mother has never recovered from the loss of my brother Pierre, who died during the Terror.

So poor Sophie had lost her brother too!

> That fiend Robespierre sent him to the guillotine along with the great Danton. They died because they tried to turn the Revolution away from violence, and toward peace and justice for all. I try to remember that, and be proud, but my heart is wrung. My younger brother Étienne has also suffered. He was wounded in battle, and had to have his right leg amputated. But at least his life was spared, and we are grateful for that. My father, like your mother, was imprisoned for a long time, and I fear he will never completely recover his health. Who could have believed at the glorious dawn of the Revolution that such sorrows would come to pass?
>
> I read in the newspapers that the royalists are becoming popular again in Paris these days. I suppose you and your friends will be glad of it. As for me, I scarcely know what to think. My father

says the present government is corrupt, and
unworthy of the greatness of the Revolution.
Certainly people here complain a lot, and some even
say it would be better to have a king again – though
they do not say it very loudly yet!

But enough of politics. I wish you to know, my
dear Pauline, that I am soon to be married to
Monsieur Édouard Lantaigne. He has been most
kind to me and my family through these difficult
times, which I will never forget. He is a doctor, like
my father, and I take comfort in that. It is time we
all were healing.

I remain, as always, your devoted
Sophie Duvernier

Have a king again! Could it be? Papa's dearest hope
had been that people's hearts would turn toward the
monarchy again, and now . . . I felt dizzy for a moment,
and put the thought from me.

"Well," I said, after a pause, "Sophie is much
changed, isn't she? Who'd have believed that a
firebrand like her could become so tame? But then,
as she says, her family has suffered. And now she's
getting married. There's a subject dear to your
heart!" For Pauline had already told me she was
engaged to be married to the Comte de Béarn in the
New Year.

"You'll be marrying soon yourself," Pauline said,
blushing.

I shrugged. "Not in here," I said. "The government won't let me!"

I picked up Coco's ball, which he had fetched to my feet, and tossed it for him. "Anyway," I went on, "I don't feel grown up enough to get married. I've missed so much ordinary life!"

"Still, there's politics to think of."

I sighed. "You're right, Pauline. If ever I do get out of this place I won't be allowed not to marry at all, or to marry just anybody. It will have to be an Austrian archduke or some prince or other, I suppose."

Pauline's eyes widened. "But surely . . . I mean, what about your parents' wishes?" she asked.

"Wishes? What can my poor parents have to do with it now?" I asked bitterly.

"But it was all planned! Her late Majesty told my mother all about it when we were first in the Tuileries. You were to marry your cousin, the Duc d'Angoulême."

Marry *Antoine*? "You mean it was settled? But Maman never told me!"

"Is that so surprising? Think how young you still were then – just eleven. You're forgetting."

"And it was all agreed upon?"

"Within the family, yes. Though Maman says the Emperor of Austria has other ideas about a suitable husband for you now."

"Oh, he does, does he?" I said, stung. "Does he think I'm a stick of wood or a cabbage he can do as he likes with?" I tossed my head. "No. If my parents wanted me to marry Antoine, then Antoine it will be!" As quickly as it had flared up, my anger cooled and I began to laugh.

Pauline put her hand on my sleeve. "Are you all right?" she asked.

I patted her hand. "Quite all right. I was just thinking of the poor monkey!" Seeing Pauline's puzzled look, I explained, "Oh, it's just a silly name I had for him when we were children."

"But why *poor*? I'm sure His Grace the Duke will be honoured – delighted – to marry you!" Pauline looked shocked. Sometimes I suspected she was more of a royalist than I was.

"I daresay he won't mind too much. But, oh, Pauline, what a mismatch!"

"Mismatch? But you are both of the royal Bourbon line."

"If you'd ever met Antoine you'd know. He's so serious, Pauline," I explained. "He needs someone more like you, not a willful minx like me. I used to make his life miserable when we were children together at Versailles. I'd tease him, spoil his games, spill ink on his books – all on purpose too. How awful I was to him."

I lay awake that night, thinking. Wondering about Antoine. Wondering if he might be wondering about me.

Perhaps he would be King of France some day, after our uncle of Provence and then Antoine's father had their turns. So if I married Antoine, I would be . . .

Queen of France!

I was so shocked that I sat bolt upright in bed. Queen of France, like my mother before me. And look what had happened to *her*.

I sank down again and pulled the coverlet right up to my chin. I didn't want to be Queen!

Did I?

My thoughts tumbled on. Antoine always cared about politics, I told myself. And he must have learned more in all these years. If he were King and I were Queen, I could make him listen to me, to Papa's ideas . . .

Could the two of us keep Papa's dream for France alive? Might the door I had thought closed forever when Charles died, be open after all?

I didn't sleep a wink that night, but it was for joy.

I couldn't wait to talk to Pauline about it the next day, but we had scarcely reached the garden when Renette came hurrying after us.

"Mademoiselle," she gasped, "your friends must leave at once. Rioting has broken out in the city. It may be difficult for them to get home safely!"

"Where is my mother?" cried Pauline, running over to the little table under the trees to gather up her hat and gloves.

"Waiting for you at the Tower gate, Mademoiselle."

"Listen!" I said. In the distance there were confused sounds of shouting, followed by a dull boom.

"Cannon!" murmured Pauline, turning pale. "The royalists must be rising in revolt."

"Go quickly," I said, hugging her. "Be careful! If you can't get through, come straight back here. We'll worry about getting permission for you to stay later."

I refused my evening meal. Huddled in a shawl, I sat listening to the shouts and cries and bursts of gunfire.

"People are being killed," I whispered to Renette. "I feel as if I'm to blame. If I weren't here, maybe they wouldn't have risen against the government."

Pauline and the Duchess arrived at the usual time the next morning. But I could see at once from their faces that the news was bad.

"It's all over, Madame," said the Duchess, sinking breathlessly into an armchair.

"The poor brave fools had no cannons, few weapons," added Pauline sadly. "Young men marched right up the streets shouting and cheering and waving white banners, and the army shot them down."

"A General Bonaparte led the government artillery. Napoléon Bonaparte. He was quite ruthless." Madame de Tourzel spoke bitterly. "I wish the government joy of him. People say he's a most ambitious man."

A terrible thought struck me. "You'll . . . you'll still be able to come to see me, won't you?" I whispered. "I couldn't do without you now!"

Madame de Tourzel looked grave. "We must prepare for the worst. All royalists will be doubly suspect now. I only pray that our correspondence with your uncle is not discovered. If it is, it will be the worse for all of us."

"Perhaps you shouldn't come for awhile, then," I said. "Maybe that way they won't suspect us."

But it was too late. At first, when they no longer came, I told myself that they were just being careful. Then a white-lipped Renette brought the news that my secret letters to my uncle had been discovered. Pauline and the Duchess had both been arrested. Now there would be a government investigation, and everyone, including Renette and me, would be interrogated.

It was like stepping back into an old nightmare. Once again I faced cold-eyed interrogators who shot angry questions at me. Who would be convicted now, and who would die?

They told me that communicating with my uncle, the Comte de Provence, was treason against the French Republic. I confessed right away that I had written to him, but I swore that I had said nothing against the government of France. But then they already knew that – they had my letters. I denied that Renette had known anything about the letters, but it was no use. They wouldn't believe me.

So my poor fox became a prisoner herself. She was no longer allowed to leave the Tower, even to visit her family.

"Forgive me, Renette," I said, miserably. "I *had* to write those letters. I just had to take the chance. But I never dreamed they'd blame *you!*"

"Oh, Mademoiselle." She burst into tears. I put my arms around her and tried to comfort her.

Pacing the empty garden, its trees now bare of leaves, I despaired. Would this be my life forever, or would I be tried for treason and executed? Were Pauline and Madame de Tourzel in prison? Would I ever see them again? And just a month ago I had felt so full of life and hope!

"You must distract yourself, Mademoiselle," Renette urged me. "The government has sent a message asking you to write down all that happened to you and your family. Why not do it?"

At first I agreed only because I thought it might help her regain favour with the government. For myself, I could hardly bear to put the words on paper. But it was true that there was no one else left who knew the whole story as I knew it. No one at all.

So I began. Sometimes I couldn't write fast enough, my pen scratching feverishly across the paper. Other times I would have to stop and bury my face in my hands, to keep my tears from blotting the manuscript. Little by little I wrote down a journal of what had happened to us and when, weaving in details I had learned later to make the account more complete. But I wrote only of events and of the fate of my dear family. The whole story, the real story, exists only in my inmost thoughts. The government had no right to my soul.

✿ ✿ ✿

I rested my head on my hands, listening to the patter of rain on the shutters. Renette came up behind me and laid her hand on my shoulder.

"It has been like living it all over again," I said, placing my hand over hers. "It was all so terrible,

216

Renette. Do you . . . do you think it had to happen the way it did?"

A long moment passed. Had I angered her? After all, her family, like Sophie's, must have supported the Revolution, or she wouldn't have been sent as my companion.

Then she said, "Do you know, Mademoiselle, ever since I came here and met you, I've asked myself the same question."

I gazed up at her, surprised.

"Oh, I don't mean that there need never have been a revolution at all," she went on. "Perhaps that was the only way to change things that needed changing in France. But it all went too far – the hatred, the cruelty, the bloodshed. Thousands and thousands of people were executed, not just your family. The Terror, we called it." She shuddered.

Yes," I said. "Yes, I know. It must have been horrible . . . horrible! But now, Renette? Is France a stronger and happier country because the Revolution happened?"

She shrugged wearily. "Right now, it's hard to say. The government is unpopular, and some of its members are dishonest. Food is scarce, and people grumble. As always." Then she smiled down at me. "But I do believe with all my heart that the ideas of the Revolution – equality and liberty for all – are great and true, and that they'll triumph some day."

I took her hand and pressed it against my cheek. "Thank you, dear Renette. It helps me to know you believe that," I murmured.

A week passed and I still had no word about my friends or of what my own fate would be. Then one grey November morning, I heard Renette running up the stairs. She burst into the room, quite out of breath.

"Mademoiselle, oh, Mademoiselle! There's someone from the government! He's on his way to speak to you."

A man entered and bowed low. I got up. My heart hammered in my breast, and the blood coursed so loudly in my ears that I could scarcely understand what he was saying. I heard in little blurts of sound, without sense or meaning.

" . . . exchange of prisoners . . . Austria . . . next month . . . His Imperial Majesty, the Emperor . . . "

I couldn't take it in. I turned to Renette. Her face was radiant!

"Help me, Renette. I don't understand," I whispered.

Her eyes shining, Renette swept me a curtsey deep enough to satisfy even the Duchess. "Your Royal Highness," she said joyously, "it is freedom!"

❧ ❧ ❧

The next weeks flew past. Never had the gloomy old Tower seen such comings and goings and plans and preparations. A *trousseau* showered down upon me – dresses of muslin embroidered with gold, gowns of satin and lace and pink velvet, furs and ribbons and laces. Renette revelled in it all, sighing in ecstasy as she unpacked the new garments, each one more exquisite than the last.

And I? I had swung so often from hope to despair that now it was hard to feel anything. My one joy was the news that Pauline and the Duchess had been set free, and were no longer in danger. I was still not allowed to see them, but I wrote eagerly to ask if they would go with me to Austria.

But, *Alas, Madame,* Pauline wrote back, *my dear mother has been made ill by our recent dangers. She is now too frail for a winter journey, and I would not like to leave her. And Monsieur de Béarn wishes our wedding to take place soon, and does not want me to go to far-off Austria.*

My dearest Pauline, I replied, *you know better than anyone how much joy I wish you. Be happy, and believe, as I do, that somewhere, sometime, we will meet again.*

So I chose other companions for my journey. Madame de Soucy, who was the daughter of my dear old macaw, and several other ladies would go with me. So would faithful Gomin, at least to the borders of France. And Hué, whose loyalty had never faltered.

But not poor Renette. I knew how much my dear fox yearned to go with me, and pleaded for permission to take her. But the Emperor of Austria would not accept any ladies who were not of the former court of the King of France.

It wasn't hard to pack my personal belongings, for they were few. My mother's gold and amber watch, a trictrac board that had belonged to Charles. The rest I gave away to Renette and the other guardians who had been so kind to me in these last months.

December eighteenth was my last day in the Tower. That afternoon, I put on my green silk gown, and wrapped myself warmly in furs. I strolled up and down the garden, bowing to the onlookers who had been allowed to gather again in the attics above for these last days.

The hours crept by. The government wanted me to leave at night, in case people came to cheer me and made a disturbance. They had told me I would be travelling incognito, under the name of "Sophie." *Sophie!* I didn't know whether to laugh or cry.

It was very late when Monsieur de Bénézech, my escort, arrived. I nodded to him, acknowledging his bow. Then I turned to Renette, who was weeping bitterly.

"Oh, Mademoiselle, I'll never forget you, never!" she sobbed.

"I won't forget you, either, dear Renette," I said, my own eyes full of tears. "And I want to give you this." I pressed the manuscript I had written into her hand. I kissed her and walked to the door, then turned and ran back for one last hug.

Outside it was pitch dark and piercingly cold. With Coco under my arm, I crossed the uneven cobblestones of the courtyard. Beyond the gate, a closed carriage stood waiting.

Images floated to the surface of my mind. Faces below a torchlit balcony . . . A daisy wreath bound with summer grasses . . . Blood-red dawn over the Seine . . . The brooding battlements of the Tower . . . Papa's spectacles lying on a map of France . . . The cold bronze smile of the goddess of Fortune . . .

"I have lived in this place for three years, four months, and five days," I said aloud. To myself I added, And I would no doubt live here longer yet, if they knew what I am about. For I am my father's daughter, and while I live, he does. I carry his message for the future of France.

As we reached the gate, the clock of a nearby church began to strike midnight, the chimes dissolving like silver ripples across the still night air. It was December nineteenth, a new day.

My seventeenth birthday, I thought. Nobody else would have remembered that!

I stopped and looked back. Behind me the dark bulk of the Tower reared upward against the winter stars, casting a long finger of shadow that fell across me in the moonlight. It would always be there, I knew. In my memories, in my dreams. But the carriage was waiting, and the roads of France lay open at last.

All my family had gone this way before me. I alone, the last of all, went to freedom.

I stepped through the gate, and out of the shadow.

Epilogue

Sometimes it seems to me that my life has been one long journey. First to the Emperor's court at Vienna. Oh, how they argued about me, for two whole years. I must marry this one or that one. I must live here or there. I must do this or that, it was my duty . . .

I wouldn't agree to anything except to marry Antoine. And that made them very angry with me.

Then that monster, General Napoléon Bonaparte, made himself Emperor of France. Everyone feared his power, and it seemed certain that my family would never return to rule France. This meant I wasn't politically important anymore. So the Austrian Emperor, no doubt tired of my stubbornness, let me go to join my uncles and Antoine in their exile.

Yes, I married Antoine. He was just as I had remembered him, my dear monkey. When I talked to him about what Papa had said, he understood, and agreed. What joy! In our darkest hours, when we had little money and no friends, we would feed our hopes by dreaming about what we would be able to do for France . . . someday.

For long, lonely years we wandered the length and breadth of Europe. Everywhere the agents of the Emperor Napoléon hounded us onward, never allow-ing us to settle down for long. How Napoléon must have feared us. He was only upstart royalty, after all! One of the first things he did was to tear down the Tower, lest people turn it into a shrine to the memory of my family. Much good that did him, for in 1814 he was defeated at last, though it took the allied armies of all Europe to do it.

Then we were summoned home to France, Antoine and I, and Oncle Charles, and Oncle Louis, who was now King Louis XVIII. It was like a wonderful dream come true.

Everywhere along the route to Paris, people flocked to catch a glimpse of us, and to cheer us. At a glittering reception in one town – I can't remember which one, I was in such a daze – I saw a tall, dark-haired woman standing modestly on the sidelines. It was Pauline! I flung myself into her arms, and we wept for joy together. I thank God for her friendship. What I wrote to her so long ago is true. I have loved her all my life.

My family settled down in those very Tuileries I once hated so much. Then in 1815 Napoléon escaped from exile. His army marched on Paris, and fools counselled the King to flee. Not I! I knew we should stand our ground. I jumped on my horse and tried to rally the troops to defend us. It did no good. Royalist supporters just packed me on a boat and shipped me out of the country. They say that when Napoléon heard that story he said, "She's the only man in her family!"

Then, thank God, Napoléon was defeated forever at the great battle of Waterloo. My uncle Louis regained his throne, and for many years all was well. My uncle realized that there was no going back to the old days. He was a constitutional king, the kind my dear Papa would have been if only they had let him live. But, oh, Oncle Louis was cold and cautious, so of course the people could not love him.

Oncle Louis died in 1824, and Oncle Charles, Antoine's father, became King Charles X. The truth is, Oncle Charles was a kind man, but he was a fool. He threw everything away. He tried to rule France as if the Revolution had never happened, and in 1830 the people of Paris once again rose up in revolt. Oncle Charles had to abdicate, and Antoine had to give up his claim to the throne too, because he was Oncle Charles's son.

And I? I was Queen of France for just ten minutes, the time it took Antoine to read the long document of abdication and sign his name below his father's. I thought then of my mother, that unhappy queen. How dearly she paid for her mistakes. And how dearly Antoine and I – and France – now had to pay for Oncle Charles's!

After that it was unending exile. We wandered to Scotland, Bohemia, Italy. At last, after Antoine died, I came here to a country house at Fröhsdorf, not far from Vienna. I have come to love it here, and that is good, for I can never go home to France again, that I know. Young Henri, Ferdinand's son and the last of our family, lives nearby. He has always been most dear to me, as if he were the child Antoine and I never had. I have been a second mother to him. And I dream, not quite daring to hope, that someday France will summon him home again to rule.

So here I sit, an old woman now. I still am not charming, though I can hardly count that as a Sorrow, for my dear friends love me in spite of it.

I like to spend part of each day sitting before one particular window in my house. My maids wonder why, but I never explain. The truth is, something in the view – the noble line of trees, the sweep of grass, the fountain – reminds me of Versailles. Where it all began so long ago. It seems to me that somehow a circle is complete, and I have a measure of peace.

I sit, and I embroider. I can almost see my old macaw nodding, satisfied with me at long last. "You see, Madame? I *said* you could do it!"

Yes.

The needle glides through the cloth, bearing its train of silk. And I make stitches of memory, stitches of time.

Eclipse Photograpy

Sharon Stewart has always been interested in writing, then "fell completely in love with History" while studying at university. When she discovered *The Journal of Madame Royale*, written by Marie Thérèse Charlotte de France, she was able to blend her love of history and writing.

Although Marie Thérèse was a royal princess, she was also someone history had almost forgotten, since she had no claim to the French throne. As Sharon learned a little about Mousseline, she realized she *had* to find out more. And when she discovered a rare uncut edition of Mousseline's journal written in French, it almost seemed that she was "meant" to write the story of Mousseline's life.

Sharon's other books are *The Minstrel Boy* and an upcoming novel called *Spider's Web*.